"You really don't *have a clue about Christmas, do you?"*

Juliet handed Nick a curly white wig and beard. "Santa has to wear a beard. It's in his contract."

Nick gingerly tried it on. "This thing itches," he grumbled, looking in the mirror. "I doubt I'll fool anyone."

"Aren't you supposed to be a master of disguise or something?"

"I flunked that class in spy school."

"What you need is more belly." She grabbed a pillow from the bed and started to stuff it down the front of Nick's trousers. As she adjusted the pillow, her face turned the same color as the costume. Nick fought back a grin. She was so cute when she was being the good girl. The well-behaved librarian.

Nick had seen the other side of Juliet. He knew that she could be as wild and uninhibited as any woman he'd ever known. She certainly turned him on a lot more, with those sexy little moans, those deep, moist kisses—

Whoa! Santa had better keep his mind on his reindeer....

Dear Reader,

Happy holidays! In honor of the season, we've got six very special gifts for you. Who can resist *The Outlaw Bride,* the newest from Maggie Shayne's bestselling miniseries THE TEXAS BRAND? Forget everything you think you know about time and how we move through it, because you're about to get a look at the power of the human heart to alter even the hardest realities. And you'll get an interesting look at the origins of the Texas Brands, too.

ROYALLY WED, our exciting cross-line continuity miniseries, continues with Suzanne Brockmann's *Undercover Princess.* In her search to find her long-lost brother, the crown prince, Princess Katherine Wyndham has to try life as a commoner. Funny thing is, she quite likes being a nanny to two adorable kids—not to mention the time she spends in their handsome father's arms. In her FAMILIES ARE FOREVER title, *Code Name: Santa,* Kayla Daniels finds the perfect way to bring a secret agent in from the cold—just in time for the holidays. *It Had To Be You* is the newest from Beverly Bird, a suspenseful tale of a meant-to-be love. Sara Orwig takes us WAY OUT WEST to meet a *Galahad in Blue Jeans.* Now there's a title that says it all! Finally, look for Barbara Ankrum's *I'll Remember You,* our TRY TO REMEMBER title.

Enjoy them all—and don't forget to come back again next month, because we plan to start off a very happy new year right here in Silhouette Intimate Moments, where the best and most exciting romances are always to be found.

Enjoy!

Leslie J. Wainger
Executive Senior Editor

Please address questions and book requests to:
Silhouette Reader Service
U.S.: 3010 Walden Ave., P.O. Box 1325, Buffalo, NY 14269
Canadian: P.O. Box 609, Fort Erie, Ont. L2A 5X3

CODE NAME: SANTA

KAYLA DANIELS

Published by Silhouette Books

America's Publisher of Contemporary Romance

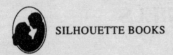 SILHOUETTE BOOKS

ISBN 0-373-07969-9

CODE NAME: SANTA

Visit us at www.romance.net

Printed in U.S.A.

Books by Kayla Daniels

Silhouette Intimate Moments

Wanted: Mom and Me #760
Her First Mother #844
Secondhand Dad #892
The Daddy Trap #922
Code Name: Santa #969

Silhouette Special Edition

Spitting Image #474
Father Knows Best #578
Hot Prospect #654
Rebel to the Rescue #707
From Father to Son #790
Heiress Apparent #814
Miracle Child #911
Marriage Minded #1068

KAYLA DANIELS

is a former computer programmer who enjoys travel, ballroom dancing and playing with her nieces and nephews. She grew up in Southern California and has lived in Alaska, Norway, Minnesota, Alabama and Louisiana. Currently she makes her home in Grass Valley, California.

For Jennie, Corey, Amanda, Alexander,
Jenna, Liam, Gabrielle and Kyle.

Chapter 1

Nick Ryan checked out the librarian.

Okay, he was spying on her.

He loitered in the biographies section, peering through the two-inch gap above the Gauguin to Houdini shelf, pretending to flip through a book on Zane Grey. The true object of his attention was over behind the front desk, checking out books, pointing people in the right direction, and with a sunny smile, greeting everyone who approached her.

The library was located in downtown Lake Andrew, Minnesota, home to sixteen thousand souls. Two days ago Nick had discovered that one of them was his brother's widow.

He couldn't exactly call her his long-lost sister-in-law, because he hadn't known she was lost. He hadn't even known she *existed,* in fact—not until that bombshell moment at the county courthouse when his scrolling finger had snagged on the entry that had revealed the jaw-dropping truth.

Bradley Thomas Ryan and Juliet Marie Hansen, married four years ago next month.

That terse, unassuming snippet of official record had swung the force of a sucker punch into Nick's gut, knocking the wind out of him. Even now, he found it hard to breathe whenever he pondered the whys and hows of the huge secret Brad had kept from him.

Maybe he would never know all the answers. But ever since Nick had had a name to attach to the pretty face in the photograph that had turned up a few months ago, he'd been determined to find out everything he could about the woman who'd been his brother's wife.

Determined? Ha! *Obsessed* was more like it. How else to explain the fact that he'd spent almost the entire three months of his unwanted leave of absence from the CIA tracking her down? He hadn't even known who she was at first. Now here he was, lurking all afternoon in the public library stacks, secretly gawking at her like a lovesick adolescent.

She was even more of a knockout in person than she'd been in that picture.

Nick assumed Juliet Ryan would be as flabbergasted to learn of his existence as he'd been to learn of hers. Not to mention her reaction to finding out her husband had been a government agent. Nick's long, frustrating search for her proved that Brad had taken great pains to keep the two halves of his life completely separate. Why should Nick turn the poor woman's life upside down, stir up her grief more than three years after her husband's death, when neither of them had anything to gain by it?

He wasn't interested in family reunions or becoming like a big brother to her or indulging in some kind of warm, fuzzy sob fest where they blubbered on each other's shoulder about what a great guy Brad had been. Nick was a loner, which suited him just fine. It was practically a requirement in the line of work he and his brother had shared. All he wanted was to satisfy his curiosity. Then he was heading back to Washington and what really mattered—his job.

But first he intended to solve the riddle of how this woman could have meant so much to his brother that Brad had partitioned his life in two and lied to the one blood relative he'd had on this planet.

Hurt? Not Nick. Just…mystified.

Juliet Ryan came out from behind the front desk, toting an armload of books. She paused to adjust an ornament on the elaborately decorated Christmas tree that towered near the entrance to the children's section.

"Hello, Billy," Nick heard her say to a passing kid. "Did you find that encyclopedia volume you needed for your homework?"

"Yeah." The kid made a face, then straightened his slouching spine. "I mean, yes, Mrs. Ryan."

Juliet winked at him. "Just think, only two more days till Christmas vacation." Her voice caressed Nick's ears with a trace of lilting singsong, probably a melodic legacy from Scandinavian ancestors.

A gap-toothed grin lit up Billy's face. "I know! I can't wait!"

"What are you going to do with all that time off?"

"Go sledding, build a snowman, skate on the lake, have snowball fights with my friends...."

Juliet laughed. "Well, if I don't see you again before the holidays, you have a Merry Christmas, all right? And say hello to your mom for me."

"'Kay, Mrs. Ryan. Merry Christmas to you, too."

As Juliet continued in Nick's direction, he decided this was a prudent time to relocate. People had always told him he bore a strong resemblance to Brad, so he'd taken great care during his surveillance not to let Juliet Ryan get a good look at his face. Nothing would catch her attention quicker than spotting someone who looked like her dead husband.

Casually he drifted over a few aisles, but not so far that he couldn't continue to observe her while she shelved that armload of books.

Nick had to give his kid brother credit—Brad had sure picked a looker. Homecoming-queen material for sure, with those daintily crafted features, that lush sweep of gleaming blond hair, those crystalline blue eyes set off like jewels by a dark fringe of velvet lashes. She had a smile that could melt an iceberg into a puddle of slush in two seconds flat.

She stood about average height for a woman, five feet six or so, but there was nothing else average about her. Even the bulky knit sweater she wore over her wool skirt couldn't disguise the evidence that her breasts were—to put it bluntly—exceptional. Nick considered himself a connoisseur of the female anatomy, and Juliet definitely earned his highest rating.

With bonus points for her legs. *Fantastic* was the only word that could do them justice, in Nick's expert opinion. From his discreet vantage point in the psychology section, he was free to lust over the smooth flex of her calf muscles every time she stretched up on tiptoe to insert a book onto the top shelf. He got an eyeful when she knelt to the lower shelves, too, since her skirt inevitably hitched up a few inches to give him a tantalizing peek at glorious, bare thigh.

Not for the first time this afternoon, a twinge of guilt jabbed him. She had, after all, once belonged to his brother. Nick had no business drooling over her.

He told his conscience to pipe down. What harm could a few R-rated fantasies do? It wasn't as if he had any intention of carrying them out. He meant to admire her strictly from a distance, to glean whatever information he could by observing her at work, at home and wherever else she went for the next day or two. That was it, period. Then he was leaving town, closing this unexpected chapter in his life for good.

Juliet Ryan would never know she'd once played the starring role in a stranger's imagination.

The mouthwatering fragrance of baking cookies greeted Juliet as she came through her parents' back door just after five-thirty. She stomped snow off her boots, stuffed her gloves into her coat pockets and rubbed her hands briskly together. The warmth and light and familiar scents of her childhood home were a welcome refuge from the frozen dusk outside.

A reassuring sense of peace enveloped her, soothing the vague uneasiness that had troubled her all afternoon. Then the drumbeat of small sneakers racing across linoleum banished her jitters completely.

"Mommy! Guess what Gramma and me are doing!"

Juliet stepped through the mudroom and intercepted her daughter just inside the kitchen. She scooped Emma up into her arms and planted a kiss on the tip of her adorable nose.

Emma patted Juliet's cheeks. Her blue eyes widened. "Mommy, your face is *cold*."

"Brr!" Juliet hugged her little girl tight and pretended to shiver. "That's because it's freezing outside."

Across the kitchen, Dora Hansen dried her hands on a dish towel and hung it by the sink. "Goodness, you look like you've just blown in from the North Pole! Come sit down. I'll fix us all some hot chocolate."

"Goody!" Emma wriggled to the floor.

"Thanks, Mom, but we've got to get going." Juliet couldn't imagine how she would ever manage without her mother to baby-sit Emma during the day while Juliet worked at the library. The life of a single mother wasn't easy, but Juliet appreciated that she was luckier than most. "Let's get your coat on, Tinker Bell. Time to go."

Emma's face fell. "But why?"

Ah, the two favorite words in her daughter's vocabulary! When Emma had entered her "why?" phase several months ago, Juliet had promised herself never to take the easy way out with "just because." Explaining the world to a three-year-old could be a challenge, though. A challenge Juliet loved.

She rustled Emma's cap of blond curls. "Because Gramma and Grampa are going to eat supper pretty soon, and you and I need to go home and cook ours."

"But Gramma and me are making cookies and they're not done yet!" Emma stamped her foot.

Juliet ushered her reluctant daughter toward the back door. "We'll make Gramma promise not to eat all the cookies before you come back tomorrow." Juliet winked over her shoulder.

Dora pressed her lips together as if she were tempted to echo Emma's protest. She spoiled all her grandchildren shamelessly, but tried her best to hold her tongue when she disagreed with a parental edict.

"It's not me you need to worry about," she retorted, primping her newly permed gray hair. "It's your father and that terrible sweet tooth of his." She patted her granddaughter's cheek while Juliet wrestled Emma's uncooperative arms into her coat. "Don't worry, honey. I won't let Grampa eat more than a couple. And if he sneaks too many while I'm not looking, why, you and I can just bake another batch tomorrow. There's plenty of cookie dough left."

Emma's lower lip stayed locked in its pushed-out position.

"Pop home yet?" Juliet asked.

"He had a meeting with the school board this afternoon, but he promised to be home for supper." Juliet's father, Carl Hansen, was two years away from retiring as superintendent of the Lake Andrew public school system.

"Give him a hug for me, then." Juliet finished buttoning Emma's coat and rose to her feet.

Light glinted off her mother's glasses as she studied Juliet closely. "Everything all right, dear? You seem in such a hurry tonight."

That uneasy feeling nudged Juliet between the shoulder blades again. "Everything's fine, Mom." What could she say? *All afternoon I had the eerie sensation that someone was watching me? That every time I turned around I got the impression someone had just ducked out of sight?*

Sounded a little paranoid. "I have been feeling kind of jumpy today," Juliet admitted. Denying it wouldn't fool her mother one bit. "Guess it's just the season," she added lightly. "So many things to do before the holidays and all."

"Ah." Her mother nodded wisely. The sympathy contained in that one syllable meant she understood how tough the holidays had been for Juliet ever since her husband, Brad, had died, a few months before Emma was born.

This would be Juliet's fourth Christmas without him. Each year got a little easier, but she still felt a dull pang of grief whenever the whole family gathered together to celebrate. Juliet's parents would be there...her brother, Tim, and his wife and their four children...Juliet and Emma. But one person was missing, would always be missing. The empty place in Juliet's heart echoed even more poignantly with loss during the holidays.

But she didn't think that explained the edgy, ominous feeling that had clung to her like a shadow all afternoon.

"I'm fine, Mom. Really." She dug out Emma's mittens. "Here, put these on, sweetie, while I tie your hood." She whispered into Emma's ear, "We'll make hot chocolate after supper."

Emma's smile broke through her cloudy demeanor like the sun. Juliet avoided her mother's eyes. "Okay, say goodbye to Gramma."

"Bye, Gramma!" Her voice was muffled by the crocheted scarf Juliet had wrapped around the lower portion of her face.

"Goodbye, honey. See you tomorrow."

"Bye, Mom. Tell Pop I said hi." Juliet took Emma's hand. When they stepped outside, the cold dashed them like a bucket of ice water. "Careful, the sidewalk's slippery." She led Emma alongside the house toward the street.

"Mommy, it's cold! Let's hurry."

"Okay, come on." She gripped Emma's hand more snugly. "I had to park across the street today."

"But why?"

"No place to park on this side." Juliet paused between two parked cars. "Look both ways, remember?"

Emma dutifully swiveled her hooded head to check for cars in both directions. "No one's coming," she announced.

"Brr! Let's go, then."

They started across. All at once Juliet's heel hit a patch of icy pavement. She let out a whoop of surprise as her feet flew out from under her.

Nick slumped in the driver's seat of his dark blue rental sedan, drumming his thumbs on the steering wheel while he watched over the dashboard for Juliet to emerge from one of the nearby houses. His job gave him plenty of practice shadowing people, but he still hated the waiting part.

Not only that, but with the car engine turned off, there was a numbing absence of heat. He tugged his knit cap down over his ears, drew up his woolen muffler to cover his nose and mouth. He'd suffered a lot worse than this and survived. But a nice long swig of Irish whiskey to warm his belly would sure hit the spot right now.

He wasn't sure which house Juliet had gone into, because he'd driven past her when she'd pulled over, then circled the block so she wouldn't suspect he was following her. By the time he'd parked where he could keep an eye on her car, she'd disappeared. From his earlier snooping, he knew this upper-class neighborhood of older, two-story homes wasn't where she lived. Hopefully her visit here wouldn't be a long one.

Through the thickening darkness he caught movement from the corner of his eye. Finally! Here she came, out from behind a house on Nick's side of the street. All he could see was the top half of her body, thanks to a concealing hedge that ran along the driveway of the house next door. She appeared to be...talking to herself? Nick made note of this eccentric personality quirk.

When she reached the front sidewalk, he could finally see all of her. Her...and the little girl whose hand she was holding.

Nick sat bolt upright and gripped the steering wheel, straining forward to confirm what he was seeing. The circuits in his brain zapped into life, whirring furiously to compute the meaning of this.

A *kid?* His brother's widow had a *kid?*

But that meant—

Hastily he rubbed a circle in the icy film on the windshield so he could get a better look while they crossed the street. The next few seconds passed in a fast-forward blur of motion.

Juliet slipped and fell onto that shapely bottom Nick had so admired earlier today. She sat still for a moment after she landed, as if the wind had been knocked out of her.

At the far end of the block, headlights speared through the gloom as a car came around the corner.

Juliet and the little girl were low to the ground in a pool of darkness that lay between streetlights. That driver wouldn't see them until the last second—if then.

Nick didn't waste any more time thinking. He acted.

In a split second he was out of the car, charging toward them like a man racing bullets.

"Mommy, why did you fall?"

Juliet fought to catch her breath. "Slipped on the ice, sweetie." The shockingly hard impact on her rear end had stunned her for a second. Not only that, but it hurt like the dickens. She hoped she hadn't broken anything.

Instinctively she'd let go of Emma's hand when she fell. She was about to reach for it again when a sudden glare blinded her. Juliet threw up her arm to shield her eyes. What on earth?

Then her shaken senses comprehended what those lights were. A car was coming toward them!

The same instant that Juliet's brain sent her muscles a panic-stricken signal to *move,* Emma flew into the air. A cry of alarm hurtled from Juliet's lungs, only to lodge in her throat as she, too, was bodily swept off the ground.

Their rescuer, whoever he was, was big. Muscular. And strong as a bull. With Emma cradled in one massive arm, he half lifted, half dragged Juliet out of the path of the oncoming vehicle. Among her whirl of instantaneous impressions was the certainty that he could have easily carried her, too, if there'd been time to hoist her up.

In seconds they reached the safety of the curb. The car rushed by about ten miles over the speed limit without slowing down.

Delayed terror collided with relief. "My God," Juliet exclaimed, panting white puffs of air. "How can I ever thank you?"

"You all right?" Maybe it was concern that made his deep voice sound so gruff. Either that, or the plaid scarf that concealed his lower face. With his back to the streetlight, Juliet could only see his outline.

"I...think so." She shifted her weight experimentally and winced. "Probably have a world-record bruise by tomorrow, but as far as I can tell, there's no permanent damage."

Just then she realized the man was still gripping her forearm as if she were dangling off a skyscraper ledge. Even through her coat sleeve, she could feel the imprint of each strong finger. He followed her glance downward, then abruptly released her.

"Here." He dug into his pocket and pulled out a handkerchief. "Your mouth is bleeding."

"It is?" She touched it, surprised. "I must have bitten my lip when I fell. It doesn't even hurt."

In an unexpectedly delicate gesture for such a big man, he dabbed the edge of her mouth with his handkerchief. Juliet recoiled—not from the handkerchief, but from the electric tingle that heated her skin when his fingertips accidentally brushed her face.

He snorted. "Don't worry. It's clean." He stuffed the handkerchief back into his pocket.

Juliet flushed. "No, it wasn't that, it was just—" Just what? Just that the odd intimacy of his gesture had caught her off guard, touched something deep inside her, reminded her of desires she hadn't felt in years? *Go ahead, Juliet, let's hear how you finish that sentence.*

Emma came to her mother's rescue. Their close call had clearly shaken her up, because she hadn't said a word for nearly two full minutes. Her eyes were round with excitement, though she didn't seem the least bit fazed at being held by a complete stranger.

She tugged her scarf below her chin, crooked her finger into the corner of her mouth and regarded him somberly. "My name's Emma Ryan and I'm three years old," she announced.

Their rescuer twisted his head sharply to stare at her. "Is that right?" He sounded like he had a fistful of Christmas tinsel stuffed down his throat.

All at once Juliet sensed a weird vibration coming from him. And every protective instinct in her body went on red alert.

Poleaxed. That's how Nick felt.

Good God, was it actually possible he was an uncle?

Not only possible, but probable, he realized when his shell-shocked brain rechecked the numbers. Three years old. Brad and Juliet had married nearly four years ago. So unless she'd been fooling around on him during those lengthy periods he would have been away from home...

Nick halfway wanted to believe that. But self-deception had never been his strong suit. His stubborn nature took an almost perverse pleasure in facing the facts, no matter how inconvenient they might be.

And the fact was, this cute, tiny, bundled-up pixie

he was holding was very likely the one flesh-and-blood relative he had left in the world.

In the glow from the streetlight, he could see she had her mother's big blue eyes. The hood of her coat had fallen backward to reveal a curly mop of butterscotch hair. While she chatted happily on about cookies or something, Nick scanned her perfect miniature features for any trace of Brad. Of himself.

He marveled that so much warmth, so much animation, so much *life* could come wrapped up in such a small package. Nick hadn't had much to do with kids since he'd been one himself. He couldn't even remember holding one before. This little girl rested light as a snowflake on his arm, yet she was a complete human being, with a charming personality of her very own.

Nick was spellbound.

Emma's mother, on the other hand, didn't appear nearly so enchanted. Suspicious, yes. She probably wondered why Nick was taking so long to hand over her daughter. Nick sort of wondered that himself.

He'd thought he'd lost Brad forever. Now, miraculously, it seemed a part of his brother lived on. Somewhere inside Nick's chest, a door he'd slammed shut for good creaked ajar on rusty hinges.

He was amazed by how hard it was to hand Emma back to her mother. Juliet practically snatched her from him. "I'll walk you to your car," Nick said.

Juliet took a step backward, clutched Emma tighter and narrowed her eyes at Nick. "Thank you for saving us," she said, studying him closely as if trying to memorize the few features visible to her for a police sketch.

It was clear she had no intention of getting into her

car as long as Nick could watch her. Smart. For all
she knew, he was some kind of crazed stalker or child
molester who would follow her home.

What she didn't know was that Nick already had
her address.

"I'm glad you're all right," he said. "Both of
you."

"Bye, mister!" Now he could see that Emma had
not only her mother's eyes, but also her irresistible
smile. "I'm sure glad we didn't get runned over by
that car!"

A chunk of the distant, frozen reaches of Nick's
heart thawed to mush. "Me, too, kid."

Emma pointed across the street. "My gramma will
give you a cookie if we ask her."

Juliet quickly cleared her throat. "This nice man
has to go now, sweetie." Hint, hint.

*Go on, Ryan, get out of here before you make her
even more suspicious.*

But it wasn't that easy. In the space of a few cat-
aclysmic moments, Nick's universe had shifted off its
foundations.

Uncle. Just five little letters, but they spelled the
difference between being alone in the world and being…connected. To another human being.

Now he just had to figure out what to do about it.

Those eyes.

Juliet was seated at the pine table in her kitchen,
mending the torn pocket of Emma's green corduroy
overalls. She wasn't making much progress, though.
Whenever her thoughts boomeranged back to this
evening's encounter with their mysterious rescuer,
such a wave of dizziness washed over her, she had to

set down her sewing and put her head between her knees.

When the stranger had lifted his hand in farewell, another car had cruised slowly down the block, illuminating his face. Below his knit cap and above the scarf wrapped over his mouth, Juliet had glimpsed something that made her heart stop and turned her skin to ice.

Their rescuer had the exact same gunmetal-gray eyes as Brad. Her husband. Who'd died over three years ago in a plane crash.

Juliet raised her head slowly, flattening her hand over her stomach to calm the queasiness there. Brad was dead. She'd mourned him, borne their baby in the throes of grief and joy, raised their child alone. Somewhere during the last three years she'd even forgiven him for dying.

He couldn't be alive. Could he?

But his body had never been recovered from the wreckage of the plane that had crashed into the sea....

"Oh, God..." She buried her face in her hands as another surge of dizziness overtook her.

Emma skipped into the kitchen. "Mommy? Can I have some more hot chocolate, please?"

Juliet dredged up a smile. "Sure." It wasn't until she registered Emma's look of surprise that she even realized what her daughter had asked. Second helpings of hot chocolate were unheard of.

Well, now she'd promised. She went to the refrigerator, got out milk, poured some into the saucepan she'd used earlier. While she waited for it to heat, she stared some more at the coat she'd hung by the back door. For about the tenth time since getting home, she walked over and drew the piece of paper from her coat pocket.

She'd spotted it on the ground, right after the stranger with Brad's eyes had left her and Emma standing on the curb. Juliet had been in a complete state of shock, but her recent fall had made her glance down to check her footing before she carried Emma to the car.

There it was, a white rectangle visible against the dirty, trampled snow beneath it. Could the stranger have dropped it? Juliet had bent down and picked it up. It was a folded sheet of stationery from a local motel. Must have fallen out of the man's pocket when he'd pulled out his handkerchief.

Juliet studied it again beneath the bright kitchen light. Scribbled on the paper were the address of the library and a pair of numbers that corresponded to Juliet's work hours that day.

Well, at least now she knew she wasn't paranoid. Someone *had* been watching her this afternoon.

Brad?

Juliet's heart shifted to jackhammer speed just thinking about it. No, it was impossible. But sweet heaven, those gray eyes…that tall, muscular build like Brad's…those disturbing vibes she'd felt from him…

"Mommy, the milk's boiling!"

Emma's cry yanked Juliet from her fog of crazy speculations. She whipped the overflowing pan off the burner, switched off the stove and reached for the phone. She couldn't stand not knowing. No matter how ridiculous, how unlikely it was, she had to find out for sure.

"Aren't you going to make my hot chocolate?"

"You can have some more at Gramma's," Juliet replied, punching out a number. "Hello, Mom? I hate to impose, but would you and Pop mind baby-sitting for a while this evening?"

The Viking Motel wasn't the fanciest place in Lake Andrew, but it was comfy, quiet and reasonably priced. It was the type of place out-of-town parents checked in to while visiting students at the local college. Christmas carols were playing over the speaker in the office.

"He left a pair of gloves at the library where I work," Juliet explained to the desk clerk. "I'd like to return them, but I don't know his name. Only that he was staying here."

"Hmm." The young woman flipped open the guest register. "What does he look like?"

"Uh, actually, I'm not sure." Juliet kneaded her forehead. Boy, did she sound like a flake! "He was tall. Big and tall. And muscular." He has my late husband's gray eyes.... "Oh, and he wore one of those leather bomber jackets."

The desk clerk brightened. "Oh, you must mean Mr. Shepherd." She closed the guest register.

"Shepherd?"

"Mike Shepherd. Room 6." Her eyes took on a dreamy glow. "Boy, what a stud, huh?"

"Er...stud. Yes." Juliet had no idea whether or not he was a stud. All she wanted to know was whether or not he was her husband.

The fact that she'd never heard the name Mike Shepherd before didn't necessarily mean anything. "Room 6, you said?"

''Out the door and to your left, about halfway down.''

''Thanks.''

Juliet emerged from the office into subfreezing air. But it was suspense rather than temperature that made her shiver. In a minute or two she would know....

For one terrified moment she debated forgetting the whole thing. ''Do it,'' she urged herself through jaws clenched to keep her teeth from chattering. ''Get it over with.''

Gingerly she picked her way along the icy motel sidewalk. Rich smells of beef stew and roasting chicken drifted over from the restaurant next door, but the mingled aromas only added to the greasy churning in her stomach.

The rooms fronted on the parking lot. Somehow she convinced her feet to carry her all the way to number 6.

Her gloved fist hovered above the door. Rapid-fire clouds of breath floated into the darkness. Her heart was pounding so hard, she could barely hear the sound when she finally knocked.

No footsteps, no flick of the curtain that Juliet could see. She fastened her stare on the tiny peephole.

The door opened.

All at once a blizzard of black dots swirled in front of her eyes. Her limbs turned to water. As her knees buckled, she heard an oath, sensed herself toppling forward.

Then, as if from a great distance, she felt herself being scooped up by a pair of arms. Big, strong, capable arms.

Arms that felt shockingly familiar.

Chapter 2

Nick glanced wildly around his motel room, searching for someplace suitable to deposit the unconscious woman in his arms. Not a chaise longue or fainting couch in sight. He hated just to prop her in a chair like a rag doll, which only left him one alternative.

Her long, silky hair shimmered over his arm as he settled her limp body onto his bed. If his hands lingered beneath her shoulders and thighs a few seconds longer than necessary, well…sue him. He'd saved her from hitting the floor, hadn't he? He was entitled to a reward for his trouble.

A few golden strands of hair had fallen across her face. After a brief hesitation, Nick gently brushed them back. Her cheek was cold, but soft as rose petals. For some reason he felt guilty—like he was taking advantage of her or something.

Then her eyelashes began to stir, along with the rest of her. Nick hastily straightened up. How the hell had she found him anyway? And what kind of story was he going to come up with to explain—

Her eyelids fluttered open. After a confused second or two of scanning the ceiling, those fabulous baby blues homed straight in on Nick.

"I'm not Brad," he said, wasting no time in setting the record straight. The shock on Juliet's face right before she'd keeled over had warned him that's what she thought. The last thing he needed was a hysterical female on his hands.

She was still in shock, judging by the frozen stare she kept aiming at him.

Nick folded his arms and leaned a little closer. "Did you hear me?" he asked, enunciating as if trying to communicate with someone who had limited English skills. "I said, I'm not—"

"Yes, I see that." She plucked each word like an overstretched guitar string. "I heard you the first time." With her elbows, she shoved herself back against the headboard into a more-or-less sitting position.

Color was coming back into her face. Red, to be specific. Nick guessed her testy tone was meant to disguise embarrassment. She didn't strike him as a woman accustomed to fainting.

Her eyes stayed fixed on him like tracking beacons. Her gloved fingers curled into the bedspread. "Who are you?" she demanded with only a slight tremor in her voice.

Nick had to admire her guts. Behind her bravado, he could tell she was badly spooked.

His well-honed professional instincts urged him to lie. But he wasn't on the job now. This was personal. And didn't she deserve the truth, after nailing him fair and square? Besides, Nick had only concealed his identity to protect her. Now it was too late.

"My name's Nick Ryan," he said. "I'm Brad's older brother."

Juliet blanched. And looked like she was about to pass out again.

Nick didn't have any smelling salts handy, so he resorted to the next best thing. In seconds he'd rustled up a clean glass and splashed in some of the Irish whiskey he'd been about to sample right before she'd knocked on his door. "Here, drink this."

She gaped at the glass as if it were a live hand grenade. "No. Uh, thank you."

Nick hesitated. "Suit yourself." He went ahead and downed a healthy slug. Something warned him he was going to need it.

"Brad didn't have a brother." Doubt and suspicion mingled in Juliet's pale, pretty features, in her voice, in every taut angle of her body. Along with a trace of fear. The fragile ledge of her jaw was fixed at a stubborn slant.

"Are you asking me, or telling me?" Nick inquired, hoisting his brows. For some reason, he couldn't resist ruffling her agitated feathers a little. Maybe it tweaked him some that she'd outsmarted him. "How'd you find me, by the way?"

She frowned as if she couldn't remember. Then, without shifting her gaze from his face, she rummaged around in her coat pocket. "I found this on the ground after you...rescued us."

Nick unfolded the piece of paper she handed him and grimaced when he recognized it. Jeez, what an amateur's mistake! Must have fallen out of his pocket when he'd whipped out his handkerchief to dab at her bleeding lip.

He crumpled the stationery and lobbed it into the wastebasket with disgust. No excuse for such a slipup, no matter how rattled he'd been at the time from discovering he had a niece.

Juliet sat up straighter to study Nick's face with a microscopic intensity that made him want to squirm. "It doesn't make sense...and yet...you do look just like him." She shook her head in disbelief. "You have the same black hair, the same square jaw, those amazing gray eyes...." She blinked as if coming out of a trance. "Well, you don't look *exactly* like him. I mean, now I can see that you aren't him, but for a second there..."

All at once it appeared to dawn on her that she was in a strange man's motel room. On his bed. She swung her feet to the floor, away from Nick, then scooted around the room as fast as those magnificent legs would carry her.

With her back against the door, she stared at him some more with those enormous blue eyes. "Why didn't Brad ever mention you?"

"Good question." Similar to ones Nick had been asking himself. He settled back against the dresser, crossed one foot over the other and took a sip of whiskey to gain himself time to come up with an answer.

"Were the two of you estranged?" Clearly she was struggling to find a rational explanation for the impossible.

"No...we were pretty close, actually." At least that's what Nick had believed until recently. He stroked the rim of his glass thoughtfully against his lower lip.

A jolt of recognition, of bewilderment, of sheer unadulterated panic skittered up Juliet's spine. Brad used to make that same unconscious gesture with his drink.

Dear God, he *must* be Brad's brother! But the implications his existence aroused were so enormous, they made Juliet's head spin. Once again, a mist of black dots peppered her vision.

Nick set down his glass and came across the room at top speed. "For Pete's sake, sit down," he said, grasping her arm and easing her into the nearest chair. "I don't want to have to catch you again." His mouth hitched with the start of a smile. "Not that I minded so much the first time."

Blood rushed to Juliet's cheeks. She hadn't stopped to consider before exactly how she'd made it from door to bed. How embarrassing, the idea that this man had carried her in his arms! Embarrassing, yet oddly thrilling in a way that both shocked and shamed her. She remembered Brad carrying her over the threshold of their honeymoon beach cottage on the North Carolina coast....

Twin arrows of sorrow and desire shot through her in a fierce assault that nearly made her gasp. Nick Ryan hovered so close, she could smell the whiskey on his breath, along with a faint masculine fragrance that smelled like an exotic mixture of sweat and leather.

His fingers were still wrapped around Juliet's wrist. Heat flowed up her arm, spreading throughout her body to melt away the last remnants of the arctic chill outside. Her skin felt charged with electricity, as if she could throw sparks off her fingertips if she only tried.

It was just because he looked so much like Brad— that was the only reason he was having such a weird, nerve-racking effect on her.

Juliet peeled off her gloves and unbuttoned her coat. It made her feel more vulnerable somehow, but she was going to swoon from the heat otherwise. Besides, it was a good excuse to extricate herself from Nick's unsettling grasp.

"I don't understand why Brad didn't tell me about you." Her mind kept snapping back to that same question.

"Seems like we're in the same boat." Nick lowered himself to the edge of the bed. His guarded gray eyes focused on Juliet with a tense alertness that reminded her of a wolf stalking its prey. "Brad didn't tell me about *you*, either."

"He didn't?"

"Nope."

"When was the last time you saw him?"

Nick calculated. "Maybe a month before he died."

A month. She and Brad had been married for six months before he'd died. Juliet drew a deep, unsteady breath. Her husband had completely misled her for some reason she couldn't begin to fathom. And he hadn't even told his own brother he was married? If she'd meant enough to Brad, surely he would have let Nick know about her. No matter what kind of rift had apparently divided them.

No. Brad had loved her. There had to be some other reason for all this. And Juliet intended to find out what it was.

"Are there any other family members I should

know about?'' she asked sharply. ''Other brothers? Any sisters? Parents?''

''Nope.''

''Aunts, uncles or cousins?''

He shook his head.

It irked her, that sympathetic look Nick was sliding her way. She didn't want him feeling sorry for her. She didn't need anyone's pity. It wasn't as if her husband had cheated on her or anything.

Juliet kept talking. She was afraid of where her thoughts might lead otherwise. ''How about family pets? Maybe a dog or cat Brad never mentioned?''

Nick's rugged features shifted to convey something close to amusement. ''Not even a goldfish.''

''Where did the two of you grow up?''

''Oh...'' He gave a vague flip of his hand. ''All over the place.''

''When did your parents die?''

His expression shuttered. ''Years ago.''

''Brad told me his mother and father were killed in an accident.''

''That's right.'' No hesitation, but a small muscle flickered along his jaw.

Frustration drove Juliet to her feet. ''You're even more closemouthed than your brother,'' she exclaimed. ''What kind of family do you come from, where no one talks to each other?''

Nick stood, picked up his whiskey, drained the glass. Though he carefully kept his face neutral, Juliet could tell she'd struck a nerve. Right away she was sorry. Even if she was upset, that was no excuse for insulting someone's family.

Automatically she dropped a hand to Nick's arm in apology. Through the sleeve of his sweater, muscles steeled beneath her fingertips. Brad had possessed this same lean, hard strength. Juliet had never felt him tense with resistance to her, though.

The wool was pleasantly scratchy against her skin. So unknown yet so familiar, the terrain of this man. Like visiting a much-loved place that had changed dramatically over the years. Juliet was intrigued by the subtle differences between this brother and the one she'd once loved...married...created a child with.

A throb of yearning quickened inside her. She let go of Nick, forced herself to look away from those probing, slate-colored eyes.

"Why don't you come to dinner tomorrow night?" The invitation was out before Juliet even realized she was considering it.

"Dinner?" He seemed taken aback by the idea.

"Nothing fancy. I've got the ingredients for beef stew—er, you're not a vegetarian, are you?"

His mouth twitched. "No."

Juliet sensed an untamed current beneath his civilized demeanor, a wildness that hinted at violence, a primitive sensuality that called out to some ancient instinct inside her.

Good grief, what was the matter with her?

Brad hadn't made her feel like this at all. Brad had been kind and gentle....

"Thanks," Nick said. "That sounds great."

"Hmm?" It took her a second to remember they'd been discussing dinner. "Oh. Well, good." She scooped up her purse from where she'd dropped it beside the door. "I'll write down directions. Will six o'clock be all right?"

"You don't need to—uh, yeah. Six will be fine."

She scribbled her address and phone number on

one of those scraps of paper that were always floating around her purse. "Here." It was hardly Juliet's habit to invite complete strangers to her house, but after all, he *was* family.

Besides, she had a plan to soften him up with a nice home-cooked meal...and then pry some answers out of him.

Right now she was so overwhelmed with questions, she needed a chance to sort them all out. And being cooped up in this motel room with Nick was a bit...unnerving. Unseemly, even. What with the bed right there and all.

His fingers brushed hers when he took her address. That mysterious tingling ignited her nerve endings again. Like an itch she couldn't quite reach to scratch.

She was allergic to him—that was it.

It was definitely time to get out of here. "See you tomorrow night, then." Juliet beat him to the doorknob. Just before she turned it, a question occurred to her. A safe one that had nothing to do with Brad, held no connection to their marriage, stirred no troubling implications.

"Why were you spying on me?" she asked. "Instead of introducing yourself."

Nick's dark pupils dilated in surprise. Those gray eyes didn't give much away, but Juliet could see they held the truth when he finally answered.

"I didn't want to hurt you," he said.

"Hurt me—how?"

He kneaded the base of his neck and sighed. "Brad's been dead over three years. I...didn't want to stir up your grief."

An impulse nearly moved Juliet to reach up and soothe away his tension with her fingers. Pure reflex.

How many times had she massaged Brad's neck for him?

"You mean you were afraid it would make me sad to see you, to be reminded of Brad?"

His hand stilled for a second. "Yeah."

Maybe so. But there was more Nick wasn't telling her, of that Juliet was certain. And tomorrow night at dinner she intended to find out what it was. All of it.

She cracked open the door, admitting a wedge of cold air that gave her goose bumps. "You were planning to leave town, then, without ever talking to me?"

Nick shrugged. "I wanted to figure out the best way to approach you first. So that it wouldn't be such a shock."

She chewed her lip, puzzling it out. "Then you already knew that Brad had never told me about you."

There was that reluctant, taciturn shift of his jaw again. "Let's just say I suspected as much."

An ominous prickling crept over Juliet's flesh. Not goose bumps this time. But the foreboding chill that it might have been better if Nick *had* left town before she'd ever come face-to-face with him.

She hugged her coat tighter and stepped outside.

"I'll walk you to your car." Nick reached for his jacket.

"No, please," she said with a touch of alarm. "I don't mean to be rude, but I'd rather you didn't." She just wanted to get away from him. Now.

"Whatever you say."

Juliet started down the sidewalk.

"One thing I'd like to know, though, before you go." Nick's voice made her turn around. He stood in the doorway, his broad shoulders blocking the opening.

"Yes?"

His knuckles tightened on the doorjamb. "Emma."

Apprehension leapt inside Juliet.

"She—she is my brother's child." Nick cleared his throat. "Isn't she?"

Immediately Juliet sensed a storm of new complications heading her way. How much safer, how much smarter, how much easier it would be to lie.

She couldn't. "Yes, of course." Her reply floated between them on white wisps of air, too late to snatch back now. "She's your niece."

A measure of tension ebbed from Nick's stance. His eyes lost their focus, as if he were seeing something far, far away. Or some*one*. "Till tomorrow," he said absently. "Six o'clock."

When Juliet reached her car, she threw a furtive glance back toward his room. Nick was still standing in the doorway, even though he must have been freezing. It was too dark for Juliet to be sure what he was looking at.

She was halfway to her parents' house to retrieve Emma when something dawned on her. If Nick hadn't even known she existed, then how had he found her?

Or perhaps even more important than how...*why*?

During the day, the lake near Juliet's house was visible from her front yard, through the stark, bare branches of the cottonwood trees that lined the streets in her neighborhood.

Nick only knew that because he'd cruised by here once before, in daylight. It was dark when he pulled up to the curb at exactly one minute past six. And the only view from her yard was the glitzy Christmas display festooning the house across the street.

He strode up Juliet's neatly shoveled front walkway. The house was one-story, brick, with white painted trim. Icicles clung to the eaves, and the bushes along the front wore eyebrows of snow. The windows had shutters. The shutters had little hearts cut out of them.

Nick still couldn't believe Brad had once lived in this Norman Rockwell painting.

He rapped with the brass knocker and tried to ignore the jittery anticipation simmering in his blood. For cryin' out loud, you'd think he was on some CIA assignment, about to infiltrate an enemy stronghold or go up against a potential assassin!

He was just here to eat, that was all. To straighten out this mess with Juliet. To see her little girl again.

His pulse kicked up its pace.

Juliet opened the door. Nick hadn't heard any approaching footsteps, so maybe she'd been lurking behind it the whole time, counting to ten before she opened it.

"Hello!" She welcomed him with a warm hostess smile that seemed just a wee bit forced. "Please, come in."

He did. "Hope I'm not late."

"Right on time."

Conventional pleasantries. A little social oil to lubricate an awkward situation.

"Smells good in here." It did, too. Rich, tantalizing aromas floated out to greet him. Must be the famous beef stew she'd promised. "I brought a bottle of wine."

Her delicate brows lifted. "Wine?"

Nick drew the bottle from the sack and handed it to her. "Cabernet. Hope that's all right."

"Um…" She studied the label.

He thumped the heel of his hand to his forehead. "Sorry. I should have asked if you drank wine.…"

"No, no, no—that's okay! I do drink wine. I mean, I used to. It's just that…" She blew a flustered stream of air through her lips and gave Nick another smile. A real one this time, one that softened her mouth and made her eyes sparkle.

He could get used to Juliet's smiles. Real quick.

"The truth is, I don't get much chance to drink wine anymore," she explained. "Without another adult to share it. Because if I opened a bottle by myself, it would just go bad before I finished it, so…this will be nice. Thank you."

"You're welcome." Man, she was pretty! Tonight her glossy blond hair was woven into a thick braid that hung down her back, with loose wisps framing her fine porcelain features. A pair of tiny gold earrings winked at Nick from her earlobes. The royal blue high-necked sweater she wore with her tan slacks deepened the color of her eyes.

As for what that nice fuzzy sweater did to her breasts, well, words escaped him.

"Please, take off your coat. Let's go in and sit down."

Nick followed her from the entryway into the living room, trying not to notice the natural sway of her hips. Here, inside Brad's house, he felt even guiltier ogling Brad's wife.

"Make yourself at home, while I check on the stew. Oh!" Juliet paused and glanced dubiously at the wine bottle. "Would you like some of this right now?"

"I'll wait, thanks."

"I'm sure I must have a corkscrew around here somewhere...." She hurried off through the adjoining dining room.

Nick looked around, absorbing his surroundings with a speed and eye for detail that were born of long practice. Cozy. That was the only word for this place. Big comfy sofa cushions, wooden rocker, patchwork pillows. Doodads and knickknacks arrayed on every horizontal surface in the room. Seemed to Nick like a lot of stuff to dust.

He swiped a finger over a ceramic figurine and checked. No dust. No surprise.

He wondered if the recliner chair had been Brad's.

He spied a framed photo on the coffee table and reluctantly picked it up. A weight settled in his chest, making it hard to breathe. It was a wedding picture. The standard beaming, slightly self-conscious pose. Brad wore a tux, Juliet a gauzy white confection of lace and silk. She looked like an angel.

Nick had never, ever seen that expression on his brother's face in his entire life. Brad looked positively...lovestruck.

It was like gazing into the face of a stranger.

Nick set down the picture harder than he'd intended. There were tons of other pictures all over the place, he noticed now. Some of Brad, some of Emma and Juliet. Most of people he didn't recognize.

He strained his ears, but all he could hear were what he assumed were typical domestic noises coming from the kitchen. Didn't kids generally make a big racket? He wondered where Emma was. Maybe helping her mother.

"Oh!" Juliet clapped a hand to her heart when Nick poked his head into the kitchen.

"Sorry." He came all the way into the room. "Didn't mean to startle you." No Emma in here, either.

"That's all right." Her cheeks were pink, either from surprise or from the steam rising from the fragrant pot whose contents she was stirring. She set the lid back on. "I just didn't hear you coming, that's all."

Nick's stomach growled. That stew smelled terrific. "Is it, uh, past your little girl's bedtime already?"

"Goodness, it's barely after six!" Juliet opened the oven and bent over to pull out a pan of browned rolls. "Emma would put up quite a fuss if I tried to put her to bed *this* early."

"Then…"

Juliet set the pan on top of the stove with a bang. The amusement vanished from her face. "Emma's visiting my parents this evening." She looked Nick straight in the eye. "I thought it would be easier for us to talk without her here."

"Yeah. Sure. You're right." Why, then, this twinge of disappointment that he wouldn't be seeing the little girl again tonight?

What Juliet had told Nick was true. It just wasn't all of it. But she wasn't about to explain that some maternal sixth sense had cautioned her to keep Emma and Nick apart—at least for now. And Juliet *never* ignored mother's intuition.

She finished tossing the salad. "Ready to eat?"

"Starved."

Juliet was afraid she wouldn't be able to eat a bite, what with the nervous churning in her stomach. She'd barely slept a wink last night, not with all those question marks circling behind her eyelids, all those doubts whispering in her ear until she was ready to bury her head beneath the pillow to drown them out.

By the end of this evening, she would have her answers. Unfortunately that didn't make her feel much better.

"Please, go ahead and sit down." She'd set the dining room table hours ago. Everything was ready.

"Can I carry anything?"

"Um…sure." She stuck the salad bowl into Nick's hands. "Oh, and the wine."

"Did you find that corkscrew?"

"Here."

As soon as Nick left the kitchen, Juliet hunted up a couple of wineglasses from the back of her cupboard, hastily dusted them off and held them up to the light to make sure they passed inspection. After a couple of trips, all the food was on the table.

"Okay if I sit here?"

"Of course."

Nick seated himself at the same place where Brad used to sit. Juliet and Emma usually ate at the breakfast nook in the kitchen. Sitting across from Nick, with his strong resemblance to her husband, was such a poignant reminder of what she and Brad had once shared that Juliet's throat closed up for a moment.

She watched in silence, fists clenched in her lap to keep them from trembling, while Nick's big, capable hands opened the wine. Stop comparing him to Brad, she scolded herself. He isn't Brad. Brad is gone. Fantasizing that Nick could ever take his place isn't fair to either one of them.

Whoa, wait a second! Juliet dug her nails into her palms. She wasn't fantasizing about Nick that way. Okay, so the man happened to be tall, dark and handsome. Big deal. So what if he positively oozed sex appeal, that his mysterious, taciturn, vaguely dangerous air would probably drive most women crazy with desire?

Juliet wasn't most women. Her only interest in Nick was what he could tell her about her late husband. He was practically family, for heaven's sake! It would be almost indecent to dream of being swept off her feet by those strong, muscular arms....

Nick poured their wine, raised his glass. "Here's to...long-lost relatives."

Juliet managed not to slop any wine on the tablecloth as she clinked her glass against his. Already she felt slightly tipsy from the fragrant fumes. Nick's eyes met hers above the rims of their wineglasses. So familiar, yet so intriguing...

Juliet took a small sip. Whether or not she wanted to admit it, the ripple of heat that slid down her throat, flowed through her stomach and made her toes curl had nothing to do with the wine.

"Mmm," she murmured politely. "Delicious."

Confrontation was alien to Juliet's nature. She'd always believed that old saying about catching more flies with honey. Or, in this case, with beef stew. Despite her nervous tension, she experienced a certain pleasure that Nick seemed to appreciate her cooking. He ate not only seconds, but a third helping of stew.

Unfortunately he wasn't nearly as enthusiastic about providing information. Though Juliet asked a number of leading questions about his and Brad's past, Nick's answers were as evasive as they'd been last night. Somehow he even managed to turn the conversation around so that Juliet was telling him about her job at the library, about Emma, about her family.

By dessert, she realized she was going to have to adopt a more direct approach.

"Mmm, this is good." Nick shoveled in apple pie with the same gusto he'd demonstrated toward the beef stew.

"Thank you." Juliet nibbled a tiny bite. "The crust didn't turn out as flaky as I would have liked, but—"

Nick abruptly set down his fork. "You mean you baked this pie yourself?"

"From scratch, yes." Juliet swallowed a giggle. He was staring at her as if she'd announced that she'd hand-built a nuclear reactor in her backyard.

"No wonder it's so good." He stared at his plate. "I think this is the first homemade pie I've ever eaten."

"Really? You mean none of your girlfriends ever baked one for you?"

Nick appeared startled by the notion. Almost as startled as Juliet was to hear the question come out of her mouth. Why on earth should she be curious about Nick's old girlfriends, when for all she knew, he had a wife and six kids stashed away somewhere?

He snorted. "Let's just say none of my old girlfriends were exactly what you'd call the domestic type." He picked up his fork and dug into his pie again.

"What about your mother? Didn't she ever bake pies or cookies for you and Brad?"

Nick's mouth tightened as if he'd bit into a sour apple. "Our mother was too busy to cook."

"Too busy? Doing what?"

He hunched a shoulder. "Digging for relics of ancient civilizations."

Juliet blinked. "Excuse me?"

"She was an archaeologist."

"An *archaeologist?*" Juliet's mouth dropped open. Nick might as well have announced that his mother had been an astronaut. Brad had never even hinted that his mother had been a scientist.

Suddenly Juliet couldn't stand all this secrecy anymore. She was tired of the verbal maneuvering, the polite conversational prodding that was getting her nowhere. She didn't intend to settle for the few crumbs of information Nick was willing to dole out.

She'd invited him here so she could learn the truth, and by God, she was going to hear it. No matter how difficult it was to listen to.

She threw her napkin onto the table. "Fair is fair."

Nick's dark brows lifted in surprise.

"I've invited you into my home, cooked dinner for you and told you all about myself. Now it's your turn."

His eyes turned wary as he swallowed his last mouthful.

"It's payback time." Juliet took a deep breath and blurted out the rest of it before she lost her nerve. "Tell me what you're hiding about my husband."

Chapter 3

Over the years, subterfuge had become second nature to Nick. In his line of work, truth was an elusive, precious commodity. You didn't freely toss it around like fistfuls of confetti at a parade. And you certainly didn't offer it without getting something in return.

True, he'd just eaten the best meal he'd had in years. But it wasn't Nick's pleasantly stuffed belly or the mellow buzz from the wine or even Juliet's homemade apple pie that made him decide to tell her the truth.

It was his own strict code of justice. The way Nick figured it, Juliet had been deprived of something that rightfully should have been hers. The truth. She'd had it stolen from her, even though she hadn't known it till yesterday.

Didn't honor and decency demand that whoever possessed it, share it now?

Nick picked up the wine bottle. "Want to help me polish this off?"

"No." She spoke through clenched teeth, as if trying to keep her chin from quivering. "What I want are some answers."

"You deserve them." He poured the last of the wine into his glass. Not the response she'd expected, judging by the way her eyes got bigger all of a sudden. "Do you want to…I mean, can I help you clear the table first?" Seemed like that might be important to her.

"No. It can wait." Juliet pushed back her chair. "Let's go into the living room."

Her long, thick braid twitched between her shoulder blades as she walked, appearing to mimic her inner agitation. She sat down in the rocker. Probably her favorite chair, a place where she normally felt comfortable and secure. She certainly looked natural sitting there. Except that she was gripping its curved arms as if bracing for an earthquake.

Nick was about to sit on the couch, when he realized that would put Brad and Juliet's wedding picture right in his line of sight. He decided to stay on his feet, selecting a position where the photo was out of vision range.

"The first thing I want to know," Juliet began, "is how did you find me? Since you claim you didn't even know I existed." Her voice wasn't a hundred percent steady, but it was determined, with a skeptical note running through it.

Nick drained his glass, set it on the coffee table. "I'll show you." With reluctance, he drew out his wallet. They were about to cross the line of no return here. Once Nick had enlightened her, Juliet would never again be able to seek refuge in the blissful shelter of ignorance.

He pulled the snapshot out of his wallet and studied it with some of the same bewilderment he'd felt the first time he'd laid eyes on it. A few of his questions had been answered since then. But there were plenty left.

Juliet wasn't the only person who didn't understand what Brad had done.

"This picture came into my possession a few months ago." Nick handed it to her.

She accepted the photo with the caution of a snake handler. "It's me," she said, surprised. As she examined it more closely, a shimmer of tender emotion crossed her face. She pressed her fingertips to her lips as if to hold back a sob. "This was taken on our honeymoon," she said in a muffled voice. "We spent three days at the beach on the coast of North Carolina."

The tenderness hardened. "What does that mean, 'came into your possession'? You inherited it? Someone mailed it to you anonymously?" The suspicion was back in her voice.

Nick shook his head. "Neither."

"Well?"

He dragged a hand through his hair and sighed. It was tough, this honesty business, when habit cautioned him against saying too much. But who was he trying to protect? Brad was dead. And Juliet's peaceful existence had already been undermined.

She was going to get hurt no matter what Nick told her. And there was absolutely nothing he could do about it.

He propped an elbow on the back of the recliner

chair. "Not long before Brad died, he left this picture of you with a...mutual acquaintance."

"Who?"

"A guy who owned a newsstand I used to stop by every morning whenever I was in town."

Her brows stitched together. "Town? What town?"

"Washington."

"D.C.?"

"Yeah."

Juliet tugged on one earlobe. "So you live in Washington."

"Just outside, actually."

"And every day you buy a paper at this newsstand."

"Well, I used to. Till three years ago, when the owner died of a heart attack."

Juliet flinched as if she'd been personally fond of old Pasquale herself.

Nick had learned long ago to steel his heart against other people's misfortunes. You either did that, or got your heart ripped out of your chest one little piece at a time.

"Three months ago," he continued, "a woman came to see me. The widow of the newsstand owner. She'd decided to move to Florida recently, and while she was sorting through her late husband's stuff, she found that picture." Nick pointed at the snapshot in Juliet's hand. "With it were written instructions to pass it on to me if Brad...didn't come back within two weeks. The old man died, you see, before he had a chance to deliver it."

Twin brush strokes of scarlet painted Juliet's pale cheekbones with color. "Why would Brad have given this man my picture?"

"I assume Brad wanted me to find you if something happened to him." Nick shook his head. "He sure as hell didn't make it easy, I'll tell you that. I couldn't spot one single clue in the photo itself. It took me months to track down the film developer, to trace it here to Lake Andrew, and even then I still didn't know your name—"

"That's not what I meant." Juliet began to rock the chair back and forth. "Why would Brad have made arrangements that would lead you to me? What made him think he might not come back from his business trip?" *Creak, creak.* The rocker went faster. "A premonition of danger? How could he have suspected his plane was going to crash?"

A plane crash, Nick thought. So that's what they'd told her. "When you say business trip," he asked cautiously, "what business are you referring to exactly?"

Juliet abruptly stopped rocking. "What do you mean, what business? *Brad's* business. His import-export company."

Oh, boy.

"Brad, uh, didn't own an import-export business." God, he hated doing this!

Juliet stared as if he'd slapped her. "What are you talking about? Of course he did!" The rocker started up again. "That's where he was when he was killed— on a buying trip to Africa. The plane went down over the ocean...." She rocked faster. "There weren't any survivors." Faster. "They never even found the wreckage."

"Who told you that?"

"Why, the State Department! They notified me several days after the crash—" Her voice broke on the last word. She swallowed, regained control. "Brad never called me while he was away on one of his trips, you see. Because he always went to remote areas where the phone service was bad. So I didn't even suspect anything had happened until he didn't come home...." Her eyes brimmed with tears. "It was a very small plane. That's why it didn't make the newspapers."

Nick sat on the edge of the recliner. He leaned over and pried one of Juliet's hands off the arm of her rocking chair. Her fingers were ice cold between his. "The State Department told you it was a plane crash," Nick said as gently as he knew how, "because they wanted to hide the real circumstances of Brad's death."

Juliet's hand jerked. "What are you talking about?" She tried to tug her hand away. Nick held on. "That's absolute nonsense," she scoffed. "This was someone from the United States government who told me what happened. Are you suggesting the government would *lie*—"

Then in her eyes he saw a horrified glimmer of comprehension, a struggle between possibility and denial. Denial won, for now.

Juliet shot to her feet. "Are you implying Brad was involved in some kind of criminal activity?" She wrenched her hand from Nick's. "Because if you are, that's completely absurd. You didn't know Brad at all if you think he was capable of drug smuggling or— or gunrunning, or *any* kind of shady dealings." She hoisted her chin and aimed a disdainful look at Nick. "Brad was a good man, a wonderful man. He was completely honest. He would never have gotten tangled up in any kind of illegal activity. Never."

An unfamiliar, vaguely annoying sensation crept under Nick's skin. It took him a few seconds to identify it as envy. He'd met a lot of women in his life, but he'd never known one who would defend him with such passion, such conviction, as Juliet displayed for Brad.

His brother had been a lucky man.

Then cold, hard logic returned. Lucky? How could a dead man be considered lucky? Resentment nudged aside Nick's envy. By marrying Juliet and pretending to be something he wasn't, Brad had left behind a big mess when he died. And fixed it so Nick would be the one forced to clean it up.

He grasped Juliet's shoulders. Her bones felt fragile beneath his hands. But he knew she possessed an inner strength that had seen her through the loss of a husband and the struggle of raising a child alone. A core of courage and determination and resilience that would help her survive what he was about to tell her.

"You're right," he said. "Brad wasn't a criminal. But he wasn't a businessman, either."

Every muscle in her body was tensed against him. Those incredible blue eyes, aiming straight at Nick like accusations....

"Brad...worked for the government." Jeez, why couldn't he come right out and say it? Dishing the truth out in bits and pieces would only prolong Juliet's torment. He just felt so damn guilty, destroying her illusions like this.

"No." Her braid whipped from side to side as she shook her head. "You're mistaken. Brad owned his own company. He didn't work for anyone else. Certainly not for the government."

Nick felt like he was about to kick a puppy. "Actually, he worked for the CIA."

Juliet froze. Her lips parted in shock. With all the color gone from her face, she might have been a marble statue beneath Nick's hands. Except for the swirling turbulence in her eyes.

"A spy?" she finally managed to gasp. "Are you trying to tell me my husband was a *spy?*"

"Well, that's not the official job title we use, but—"

"*We?*" She cocked her head as if she couldn't possibly have heard him correctly. "Are you telling me you're a spy, too?"

Every moment of Nick's training and experience, every ounce of self-preservation urged him to deny it. "That would be the commonly accepted term for it, yes."

"A spy." She said it the way she might have said "A martian". "Both of you. Spies."

"Right. I mean, it's not quite like in the movies, but—"

To Nick's utter astonishment, Juliet burst out laughing. Once he released her, she practically doubled over with amusement. Under other circumstances he would have enjoyed the musical trill of her laughter, the dazzling warmth of her smile, the charming twinkle in her eyes. Her nose crinkled up the cutest way when she laughed....

But it was hard to appreciate the fetching picture she made when he figured it was due to hysteria.

"Come on. Let's sit down and talk about this." He used his best talking-someone-off-a-ledge voice.

But when he tried to take her arm, Juliet backed

away. "That is the funniest thing I've ever heard," she said between giggles. "Spies."

She sure didn't *sound* hysterical.

"I know it must come as a shock—"

"Spies in Lake Andrew." She chuckled, then snapped her fingers. "Gosh, wouldn't that make a great title for a novel?"

It was starting to bug Nick, the fact that her amusement came at his expense. She was the one who'd insisted on the truth, wasn't she? And now that he'd finally given it to her, all she did was laugh at him.

The snapshot he'd shown her had fallen to the floor. Nick picked it up and tucked it back into his wallet. "So, did you ever actually see this import-export company Brad supposedly owned?" He leaned casually against the back of the recliner and folded his arms.

Juliet's smile wavered. "His office was in New York."

"New York? Seems like kind of a long commute from Minnesota."

"He—we talked about relocating it here, but all the big buyers are in New York. That's where all Brad's contacts were, too." By now her smile had evaporated completely. "He kept an apartment in New York. To stay in while he was there on business."

Nick spread his hands. "Why didn't you just move to New York?"

"Because my family's here. Brad knew how close I was to them."

"But you did see his New York office. I mean, you must have been there at least once." Nick arched his brows.

Juliet plucked absently at her gold earring, a little

nervous tic he was coming to recognize. "Well, no, actually. I mean, that's where we met, in New York. While I was there for a library seminar."

"And Brad never took you to see his business?" Nick let a hint of skepticism creep into his voice.

"Everything happened so fast," Juliet exclaimed. "We met, we fell in love, I only had a few days before I had to fly home. Brad said he didn't want to waste any of our time together with anything connected to work."

"I see." Nick scratched his chin. "He must have brought some of his work home with him, though. Lots of paperwork in that kind of business. And he could certainly make work-related phone calls from here. You don't need to be in New York to make phone calls."

Juliet twisted her hands into a knot. "Our time together was special because Brad was away on business so often. He refused to let work intrude on our home life."

Nick felt like a heel. But what choice did he have? Too late now to retreat. Better for Juliet to confront the unpleasant truth, deal with it and move on, rather than be tortured with doubts for the rest of her life.

"Brad obviously loved you a lot." There was that itchy, envious feeling again. Nick ignored it. "I'll bet he rang up quite the phone bill, calling you constantly from overseas."

Juliet's gaze darted frantically back and forth. Not as if she were searching for something, but as if she were trying to avoid seeing it. "Brad imported lots of native crafts made by villagers in remote areas. Most of those places didn't have telephones. Even when they did, it was very difficult to call out of the country."

"He'd have to be in major cities sometimes, though. He must have called you from airports, hotels...."

"Oh, yes!" Relief smoothed some of the furrows from her forehead. "Yes, he'd call me once in a while, whenever he could."

"He probably left you his itinerary, so that you could contact him, too."

Warily Juliet replied, "His schedule was so uncertain, it was easier for him to call me. Because he knew pretty much when I'd be home."

"What if an emergency came up and you needed to reach him? Surely you had a list of the hotels where he'd be staying, so that at least you could leave him a message."

"He—he never knew ahead of time exactly where he'd be staying." She was talking faster and faster. Nick knew he was no longer the person she was trying to convince. "Some of the countries Brad visited had very unstable economies, so hotels were always going bankrupt, new ones starting up...it made sense for him to wait till he got to the city where he'd be staying to find a hotel."

Nick forced himself to go on, despite the panic that had begun to flicker beneath her stubborn expression. "Ever have any problem contacting Brad while he was staying at his apartment in New York?"

Her lips barely moved. "He had an answering machine. He always called me back."

"Not right away I'll bet."

"He worked so hard, sometimes he forgot to check his messages for several days!" There was an undercurrent of pleading, of helplessness in Juliet's voice that twisted in Nick's gut like a dagger. That wounded, vulnerable softness in her eyes made him want to bundle her into his arms, to shelter her safe against his chest where he could shield her from the harsh reality she was trying so desperately not to face.

But he wouldn't be doing either one of them a favor.

"Juliet..." That dagger plunged deeper into his gut. "Brad lied to you."

She fell back a step, as if Nick had taken a swing at her. For an instant she swayed a little. He braced himself to catch her if she toppled. But then that inner strength took over.

Nick marveled at the loyalty that enabled her to lift her head and straighten her spine. "I think you'd better go now." He sensed the chill from several paces away.

"Juliet—"

"I invited you here for dinner because you're Brad's brother, and all you do is try to tear down his memory with this ridiculous story about being a spy."

"I'm only trying—"

"I know what you're trying to do." Her fists clenched at her sides. "You're—you're angry at Brad because of some feud you were having, which is why he didn't tell you we were married. And you're still trying to get even with him after he's dead, when he's not even here to defend himself."

Nick flung up his arms with exasperation. "Brad and I weren't feuding! Look, the reason he didn't—"

Juliet actually clamped her hands over her ears. "I don't want to hear any more of your lies." She removed one hand long enough to point toward the door. "Get out." She covered both ears again. "Please. Get out!"

A tear trickled down her flushed cheek. Nick had never hated himself as much as he did at that moment. Guilt and frustration gnawed at him, made him want to haul back his fist and punch someone.

He clamped his back teeth together. "Will you be all right? I hate to leave you like—"

"Just go." Her hands fell limply to her sides. She drew in a long, quavering breath.

"Are you sure I can't—"

"I'm sure. Go. Please." It clearly required effort to produce each word. And still she said, "Please."

What more could Nick say? Sorry to ruin your life and run? Obviously his presence here was torture to her, not comfort.

"Thanks for dinner." No doubt she wished now that she'd laced his with arsenic. "I'm sorry. For everything."

She gave one curt nod without saying a word. She didn't follow when Nick made his way to the door, retrieved his coat, let himself out.

But he hadn't taken three steps down her front walk before he heard the thud of hurried footsteps inside and the sharp click of a dead bolt sliding home behind him.

Juliet. Locking her world against him. Except now it was too late.

"Mommy, when can I go see Santa Claus?" Emma sprawled in the middle of the kitchen floor, playing with a windup merry-go-round that Santa had given her last Christmas.

Juliet stepped around her. "Hmm? Oh. Well, not today, Tinker Bell. Maybe tomorrow."

"But why?"

Juliet barely heard Emma's question. She mumbled something in reply, but her mind was completely preoccupied with the same agitating thoughts that had kept her tossing and turning all night.

It was Saturday morning, so Juliet had the day off. Functioning on autopilot, she loaded the last of last night's dinner dishes into the dishwasher. She'd been too upset to clear the table when Nick had left. Now the sight of each plate, each glass, brought back an echo of the disturbing things he'd told her after dinner.

Brad, a spy. It was too absurd to be true. Wouldn't she have known if her own husband had worked for the CIA?

All those trips...all those times I couldn't reach him by phone...

No. She wouldn't allow such traitorous thoughts to enter her head. Brad had loved her. He wouldn't have deceived her with such a monstrous pretense, kept something this important from her.

Round and round Juliet's mind circled, just like Emma's toy merry-go-round. Getting nowhere.

She'd married Brad so fast. Less than two months after she'd met him. What did she really know about him anyway?

Stop it! You know he loved you, that's all that matters.

Why didn't he tell you he had a brother, then?

Maybe because Nick was a deranged lunatic. Stalking her, claiming he was a spy...maybe it had simply been too painful for poor Brad to talk about his mentally ill brother.

Nick didn't strike Juliet as crazy, though. Would a deranged lunatic have saved her and Emma from being run over? He was secretive, yes. Closemouthed. Evasive. But what else would you expect from a spy?

She slammed the dishwasher shut with a bang. Nick was *not* a spy. That was simply too farfetched to believe. Let alone his claim that Brad had been one, too.

Lies. Everything Nick had told her must be lies.

But why on earth would he lie to her?

A tug on her slacks drew her attention downward. "What's the matter, Mommy?" Emma, gazing up at her, an anxious look clouding her adorable, angelic features. "Your face looks all funny. Like when you see a spider."

"Oh, Emma." Juliet dropped to her knees and gave her daughter a desperate hug. "I'm sorry. I didn't mean to worry you." She pressed a fierce kiss into her little girl's silky curls. "Everything's okay. I promise."

She'd never broken a promise to Emma. Somehow, no matter how all this turned out, she wasn't going to let it affect her child.

No matter what Brad had or hadn't done, she was going to make sure that Emma went on believing that the father she'd never known was as wonderful, kind and loving as Juliet had always told her.

Reassured, Emma wriggled out of her mother's embrace and plopped back down beside her merry-go-round. For what seemed like the hundredth time this morning, she wound it up and set the gaily colored horses rotating again. Round and round, round and round. Just like Juliet's brain.

Nick could have phoned her. There was absolutely no reason why he had to see Juliet in person to give her the name of someone at the CIA who could verify that Brad had once worked there.

But it would be kind of a shame to leave town without seeing that little girl one more time. Emma.

His niece.

Nick flipped the word over in his mind again like a shiny new coin he'd found on the ground. He still couldn't quite grasp the concept.

And if he had another reason for returning to Juliet's house one more time, a reason that had to do with seeing Juliet herself, Nick wasn't about to admit it. Why should he want to see her again anyway? Their last encounter had ended with her laughing at him and essentially calling him a liar.

Maybe that was why he was so determined to prove he'd been telling the truth. He could just leave town, leave Juliet to struggle for the rest of her life with the hornet's nest of pesky doubts and questions he'd stirred up. Let her go on believing Brad had been some kind of saint, if that's what she wanted!

But it rankled Nick that she thought he would lie to her.

She was better off facing the truth. Bitter medicine, perhaps, but she ought to swallow it for her own good. In Nick's book, harboring a bunch of romantic illusions didn't get you anywhere. The trick to survival was facing cold, hard facts.

The least he could do was offer her that option. The choice would be up to her.

Nick knocked on the front door. One of the lace curtains moved, just a little. Juliet opened the door. Not very far, but she opened it. She just stood there, watching him with those injured-doe eyes, on guard against further hurt, vaguely accusatory. Like he'd let her down or something.

Damn it, he couldn't stand to have her look at him that way!

"May I come in?" he asked, since she apparently wasn't going to invite him.

"I...think we've said everything there is to say." She shifted slightly as if to physically bar his entrance. Her long blond mane was drawn back in a ponytail.

Nick was professionally trained to notice details, but anyone could tell Juliet hadn't gotten much sleep last night. Her eyes had a slightly bruised look, with lines of strain etched at the corners. Her pale skin was stretched taut across her high cheekbones. And the crazy thing was, she was still a knockout, even with her enticing curves concealed by a baggy sweatshirt and faded corduroys. A restless pull of attraction stirred inside Nick.

Fine. If she wanted to have this conversation on her front porch, in plain view of anyone who wandered by, then—

He heard a faint thumping inside the house. He didn't understand why Juliet whipped her head around in alarm until the sound grew close enough to identify as the pounding of little feet. Juliet's graceful fingers tightened on the door as if itching to slam it in Nick's face. But of course, she couldn't quite bring herself to do it.

"Mommy, who's at the door?"

"Emma, go back and play in the—"

A curly blond head popped out from behind her mother's legs. "Hi!"

Nick cleared his throat. "Hi, yourself."

"Emma, please go—"

"My merry-go-round broke." She spoke to her mother, but didn't take her eyes off Nick's face. He couldn't stop staring at her, either.

Juliet shifted, clearly trying to shield Emma from Nick. "I'll come fix it in a minute. Now—"

Emma rolled her big blue eyes. "That's what you *always* say, an' then we hafta wait for Uncle Tim to come over and fix it!"

Nick couldn't pass up this chance to get his foot in the door.

"Maybe I could fix your merry-go-round," he said.

Juliet frowned and said quickly, "That's not necessary."

"Could you?" Emma folded her dimpled hands in a pleading gesture. "Oh, could you, mister? Please?"

"I'd be glad to." Even as he smiled at her, it occurred to Nick what a rash promise he was making. What if he couldn't fix the damn thing? Then he would have to face the disappointment in her eyes.

"Goody!" She bounced up and down, her rosy cheeks wreathed in smiles. "Come on! It's in the kitchen." She grabbed Nick's hand and tugged.

Which didn't leave Juliet much choice except to step aside and let him in. She handed Nick a dirty look as he went past.

Oh, well. Considering all the excellent reasons she had to resent him, what did one more matter?

Chapter 4

Emma didn't wait for Nick to take off his coat. She towed him straight through the house to the kitchen. He couldn't get over how soft and warm her tiny hand was in his. Good grief, her little bones were lightweight as a bird's! It disturbed him to think how easily they could be crushed.

"Here it is," she announced, letting go of his hand. She dropped to the floor in a cross-legged position.

Nick joined her. "Let's see now, what seems to be the problem?" He picked up the toy merry-go-round.

"It's broke."

Nick chuckled. "Okay. Let's see if we can figure out why it's broke." He'd had to dismantle a ticking time bomb or two in his day. Fixing this should be a piece of cake.

Juliet had come into the kitchen right behind them. Nick looked up from his position on the floor. "You got a screwdriver around here someplace?"

Wordlessly she opened a drawer and handed him one. Why did women always keep their tools in the kitchen, anyway? He went to work on the merry-go-round, not sure if it was Juliet's silent hostility or Emma's enthusiastic chatter that he felt the most pressure from.

"My mommy's gonna take me to go see Santa Claus."

"Is she?" Nick pried off the base of the merry-go-round.

"Know what I'm gonna ask Santa for?"

"What's that?"

"A new doll! So I can take care of her and feed her a bottle and sleep with her every night." Emma hunched her shoulders with anticipation. "And I'm gonna call her Tinker Bell, 'cause that's what my mommy calls me."

"Tinker Bell, huh?"

"You know. Like in *Peter Pan.*"

"Oh. Right."

"And I'm gonna ask Santa for a puppy, too, only…" Emma sidled a mischievous glance in Juliet's direction. "My mommy says we can't have one, because she works all day and I stay with my gramma so the puppy would be all alone, but I really, really want one, and I've been a very good girl all year, so I think Santa will bring me a puppy if I ask real nice and say pretty please, don't you?" She clasped her hands with a beseeching, angelic expression that would have sent Ebenezer Scrooge himself rushing straight to the pet store. "Don't you think Santa Claus will bring me a puppy?"

"Uh…" Nick shot a *Help me!* look at Juliet.

She was leaning back against the counter, arms

folded like a saloon bouncer's, eyes narrowed, brows knitted together in a scowl. Wait. Could that possibly be a smile teasing up the corner of her lips?

She was probably enjoying Nick's predicament.

She gave him a quick, covert shake of her head and mouthed an exaggerated ''No.''

Thanks a lot, he thought. To Emma he said, ''Gee, last I heard, Santa had stopped bringing puppies to kids. Makes the reindeer too nervous, you know, having them on the sleigh.''

''Oh.'' Emma's expression veered close to a pout, then cleared. ''Well, maybe somebody else will give me a puppy for Christmas.''. She batted her long, curly eyelashes at him.

Hoo, boy. Tiptoeing through a minefield here.

Luckily the merry-go-round was ready for a test run. ''Let's see if it works.'' Nick handed it to Emma to do the honors.

She gave an excited little gasp, wound it up and set it on the linoleum. It rotated slowly, toy horses bobbing up and down, tinny music lifting into the air.

Emma's face lit up like a Christmas display. ''You fixed it!'' she cried. Then, before Nick could react, she scrambled to her feet and threw her arms around his neck.

He couldn't have been more stunned if she'd sprouted wings and started flying around the kitchen like the real Tinker Bell. This was a brand-new experience for Nick. What the heck was he supposed to do now?

He heard Juliet make a faint sound in her throat.

Tentatively Nick lifted his free arm and put it around Emma. He'd never hugged a kid before. Hadn't realized how wiggly and bouncy they were.

How fast their hearts beat. How they gave off heat like a miniature furnace.

He patted Emma awkwardly on the back. Such a small back! His hand spanned the entire breadth of it. He could feel each tiny sharp vertebra poking through her shirt. On impulse, just for a second, Nick held her close. A peculiar, unsettling pressure expanded behind his ribs. Relief, maybe, that she didn't break. Or oxygen deprivation. She did have her arms locked awfully tight around his neck.

Just as abruptly as she'd hugged him, she let him go. "Thank you, mister," she said, her eyes shining as if he'd just snatched the moon out of the sky and offered it to her. "Thank you for fixing my merry-go-round."

"You're welcome," Nick managed to say. She must have had him in a tighter stranglehold than he'd thought.

"Know what?" She tipped her head to one side, regarding him quizzically.

"What?"

She brought her face close to his again, this time to squint at him with puzzled curiosity. Her eyes widened. "Mommy, look!" She threw a delighted smile over her shoulder as she pointed straight at Nick's nose. "This man looks just like my daddy!"

Juliet's heart swooped. She'd been so concerned that Nick might say something to Emma, let it drop that he was her uncle, that it hadn't even dawned on her Emma might figure it out for herself.

She shouldn't have been surprised. Emma was awfully perceptive for her age, and there were photographs of Brad all over the house. From the time

Emma was a baby, Juliet had taught her to recognize Brad, through stories and pictures had acquainted her with the father she would never meet in person. *Daddy* had been the second word Emma learned how to say.

How on earth was Juliet going to explain Nick's connection to Emma's daddy, when she didn't completely understand it herself? Emma, with all her questions, all her *whys*. Except this time Juliet was full of them, too.

Seated on the kitchen floor, Nick appeared as astounded by Emma's observation as Juliet was. He scratched his head, opened his mouth, closed it. Plainly at a loss.

Well, so was she. Unfortunately, sometimes mothers had to wing it.

She knelt so she, Emma and Nick were all eye to eye. "This is your uncle Nick, Emma. He's your daddy's brother."

"He is?" Emma focused a startled glance at him. "I didn't know my daddy had a brother."

Juliet attempted a smile. "I didn't know he did, either, until yesterday."

Emma hooked a finger over her lower lip. "Is that how come he looks like my daddy?"

"Uh-huh." Juliet automatically glanced at Nick. The quick clutch of attraction she felt made her wish she hadn't. Even though she knew it was only a knee-jerk response to a man who reminded her of the one she'd loved.

"Lots of times, brothers look like each other," she explained to Emma. "Like your cousins Kurt and Kyle."

"But Kyle's bigger."

"Uh-huh. Because he's older."

Emma turned back to Nick. "Are you older than my daddy?"

Nick had been watching their exchange with all the silent fascination of a spectator at a tennis match. He cleared his throat. "Uh...yeah. I'm—I was—three years older."

"Are you bigger?"

Amusement touched his mouth. "We grew up to be about the same size actually." He winked. "But I could always beat him arm wrestling."

"You could?" Emma checked her mother for confirmation.

Juliet shrugged. "Guess we'll just have to take his word for it."

Emma tilted her head. "What's arm wrestling?"

"Here. I'll show you." Before Juliet could reply, Nick levered himself to his feet and gestured Emma to sit across from him at the breakfast nook. "Now, you put your elbow right there, and take my hand like so...." He made a big production of adjusting their positions. "Okay, now the idea is, we both try to force the other person's hand to the table, like this. See?"

Emma nodded.

Nick glanced at Juliet. "We need a referee to start us off."

"All right. Ready? Set...go!"

Nick pushed Emma's hand halfway to the table, then eased up to let her slowly force his back the other way. Both their faces scrunched with effort. Back and forth they went. Each time Nick was about to pin Emma's hand to the table, he'd let her gain the advantage again. Finally he let his arm slam backward onto the table.

"I won!" Emma bounced up and down with glee. Then she stopped. "Didn't I?"

"You sure did, kiddo." Nick massaged his big fingers with a painful wince. "Boy, you're a lot stronger than you look."

"Mommy, I won!"

"Congratulations, sweetheart." Behind Juliet's smile, her emotions were waging a tug-of-war. It had always saddened her that Emma would never know any living relative from her father's side of the family. Juliet should be rejoicing that one had miraculously turned up.

But how could she rejoice, when Nick's appearance had cast doubt on everything she'd believed about her husband, about their marriage? How could she be happy, when Nick seemed determined to tarnish Brad's memory?

What worried Juliet even more was that Nick might try to diminish Brad in Emma's eyes, too. She was *not* going to let that happen.

"Let's do it again," Emma begged. "I wanna arm wrestle some more."

"Gotta rest for a while." Nick rubbed his arm as if Emma's exertions had strained his muscles. "And I need to talk to your mother for a few minutes." His gaze turned serious when he angled it toward Juliet.

"Just once more! I wanna win again!"

"Emma," Juliet said, "please go to your room and play for a while." Her stomach fluttered nervously at the thought of confronting Nick alone. He was right, though. They needed to talk.

"But—"

"Now, Emma. Please." Juliet didn't use that tone with her daughter too often. When she did, it was effective.

Emma scrambled down from the table. Wearing a mutinous scowl, she retrieved her merry-go-round and stomped out of the kitchen.

Nick shifted uneasily, as if he felt guilty. "Hope I didn't hurt her feelings."

"Don't worry. Luckily she doesn't hold a grudge." Juliet reached for the coffeemaker. "Would you like some coffee?"

Stalling tactics. Using the pretense of hospitality to delay hearing whatever Nick had come to say. More lies, probably. So why should she be afraid?

"No coffee for me, thanks." He reached into his jacket pocket, produced a slip of paper and handed it to her. Another piece of motel stationery, except this one had an unfamiliar name written on it.

"Donald Mason," she read. "Who's this? Another one of Brad's secret brothers?"

Nick's mouth tightened. "He's someone at the CIA who can verify that Brad worked there up until the time he was killed."

The paper nearly slipped through her fingers. "Are you still trying to sell me that ridiculous story?"

"Call him." Nick's eyes, hard and flat as slate, regarded her levelly.

Juliet clutched the paper to keep her hand from trembling. "Why should I bother? Undoubtedly he's just some pal you've talked into backing up your story." She tried for a sneer. "Besides, there's not even a phone number here."

Nick towered over her when he rose from the table. Juliet backed against the counter in alarm, but all he did was reach past her and pick up the phone. "You're a librarian," he said. "I figure it'll take you less than a minute to track down the number for CIA headquarters. That way you'll know it's the real one."

What Nick said made sense. It was logical. But Juliet didn't want logic. Logic had kept her awake all night. Logic kept yanking her in directions she didn't want to go.

Her heart was thudding like mad. She wished Nick wouldn't stand so close. He made it hard for her to concentrate, when she could smell the soap from his recent shower, feel the heat rising off his body to envelop her.

For the first time, Juliet noticed a tiny jagged scar near his hairline. Souvenir of a knife fight with enemy agents? Ridiculous. Spies used guns, not knives, didn't they? More likely he'd gotten that scar falling off his tricycle as a kid.

The idea that Brad—*her* Brad—would ever have used a gun, could ever have worked in an underworld of violence and deception and secrecy was…impossible.

As if reading her mind, Nick brought his face close to hers and said, "If you're so sure of him, then why are you afraid to make the call?"

His breath was warm and smelled of peppermint. It stirred wisps of hair that had come loose from her ponytail. Juliet's gaze dropped to his lips. Another few inches and they would be practically—

She snatched the phone receiver from him. "Fine. If you insist on seeing this charade all the way through, I'll be happy to oblige you." She turned her back on him, as much to put space between them as to dial the phone. That uncanny resemblance to Brad was starting to get to her, make her imagine things she should be ashamed of.

She punched out the number of the library. "Hello, Crystal? It's me. Are you busy right this second? Oh, good. Could you please look up the phone number of CIA headquarters for me? Yes, that's right. I'm considering a new career in espionage." Juliet gave the phone a sour smile.

She drummed a nervous tattoo on the counter while she waited, intensely aware of Nick's hovering presence. He hadn't budged from his position. His tall, broad-shouldered physique seemed to crowd out some of the air in the room, making it hard to breathe.

Juliet could hardly wait to see the look on that handsome, arrogant face when she exposed him for the liar he was.

"Yes?" She grabbed a pencil and scribbled. "Thanks, Crystal." She hung up and took a deep breath. Now for the moment of truth.

As if sensing her need for space, Nick finally backed away. Not far, though. Juliet had unconsciously crumpled the paper he'd given her into a ball, so she had to smooth it out in order to read the name again.

Carefully she punched out the number Crystal had given her. Each electronic peep in Juliet's ear was one more irreversible step, a step that might be carrying her toward the brink of a cliff. Time slowed to a crawl, yet in only seconds the phone was ringing, a voice was answering.

"Don—excuse me." She tried again. "Donald Mason, please."

The operator—receptionist, whoever she was—

didn't immediately ask, "Who?" the way Juliet had hoped she would. "One moment, please."

The apprehensive churning in her stomach grew more energetic. She studied the ceiling, swept some crumbs on the counter into a little pile, noticed the window over the sink needed washing.

The one direction Juliet refused to look was Nick's.

"Mason," said a voice in her ear.

Now she found herself perched on the edge of that scary cliff she'd so tried to avoid. "Hello." Her voice sounded strange and distant to her ears. As if she were hearing it through a tunnel. "I was told you could verify for me that a man named Brad Ryan—that's Bradley Thomas Ryan—" she gulped for air "—used to work for the CIA."

Pause. Then, with a cautious voice he asked, "Would you by any chance be Brad's wife?"

No, no, it can't be true....

"Yes." Juliet forced the reply from her throat like a splinter.

The rushing in her ears made it hard to hear him. "Brad...kept his marriage a secret from the Agency. We didn't learn of your existence until after he was—after he died."

Juliet made a tiny, strangled sound.

"To answer your question, yes. Brad worked for me for eight years. He was a good man, and his death was a personal as well as a professional loss to me."

Donald Mason said some more, but Juliet didn't hear it. How could she, with the shattered wreckage of her world crashing down around her? She was dimly aware of replacing the phone receiver. Maybe she'd hung up on him.

It was true. Brad had been a spy.

It couldn't be true, but it was. Juliet felt as dazed and disoriented as if the earth had slowed, stopped, started spinning in the reverse direction. The universe had turned upside down.

"Here, sit." Nick dragged over a chair as if worried she might not make it to the table. She let him ease her into it. Better suffer his unsettling touch than sprawl on the floor in front of him when her knees collapsed.

He pulled up a chair for himself. "Can I get you a glass of water? Or something stronger?"

"No. Thanks."

Lies. All lies. Not what Nick had told her. But her entire marriage.

Juliet could hardly avoid meeting Nick's eyes, not when he was sitting directly across from her, so close their knees were touching. She half expected to see triumph, a carefully repressed smirk of "I told you so." Instead, all she saw in his face was pity. Which was even worse.

"I'm sorry."

She nearly flinched when he said it. She felt like such a fool....

"I shouldn't have come here and spied on you. I didn't mean to interfere in your life, but I did, and there's no excuse for it." Nick closed his fingers over hers. Juliet let her hand lie there like a dead fish. "But I wanted to know the truth. Who you were. Why Brad never told me about you."

"The truth." Her lips felt numb, as if she'd just come from the dentist. "Well, now you have your precious truth. And so do I." Hot tears stung her eyelids. Mortified, she felt her face start to crumple. She would *not* cry in front of Nick.

But she did.

As soon as the first tear slid down her cheek, Nick knew he was in trouble. Not because he didn't have the foggiest idea how to comfort a weeping woman— which was true. What had him worried was the way her tears touched him, the ferocious protectiveness that surged through him and made him ache to keep her safe from harm and hurt forever.

Forever. Not a word Nick normally included in his vocabulary.

He couldn't just sit here and watch the tears leak through her fingers. He was a man of action, after all. So he acted.

"Hey, now. Don't cry." He scooted his chair beside hers so he could put his arms around her. He felt a moment's resistance, but then she sort of toppled against him like a felled tree.

Nick patted her back. "There, there." He couldn't believe he'd actually said that. But what else was he supposed to say? He tried, "Everything's going to be all right." That only earned him a fresh round of sobs. No wonder. How could things ever be all right again, after Nick had basically robbed her of the man she'd thought was her husband?

Guilt settled on his shoulders. This surely wasn't what Brad had intended when he'd left behind Juliet's photo so Nick could find her. But what *had* Brad wanted? Why had he done it?

Nick stroked Juliet's hair. "Shh, come on, now." Her head rested against his chest, hands still covering her face as if she didn't want him to see her. Her shoulders shook with sobs, though they were diminishing now.

He crooked a finger beneath her chin and tilted her

head back. Gently he coaxed down her hands. Juliet wouldn't look at him. Her eyes were puffy and red rimmed. Her cheeks were blotched with misery. Tears sparkled on her lashes like tiny diamonds.

Good God, she was beautiful!

Nick tried his best to squelch the desire stirring in his loins. What kind of an animal was he? The poor woman had just had all her illusions destroyed, thanks to him, and all he could think about was getting her into bed.

"I feel like such an idiot," she mumbled into the neck of her sweatshirt.

"No reason to." And no reason for Nick to keep his arm around her, either. But he did.

Juliet wiped her eyes with the back of her wrist. "I just can't believe—" Her lower lip started to quiver again.

Nick kissed her forehead, brushed aside several loose wisps of hair that clung to his mouth. "You've had a big shock. It'll take time for it to sink in."

"This will never sink in." Juliet shook her head. "Brad. A spy. Living a double life." She clenched her fists in her lap. "And me too stupid to figure it out."

"You're not stupid."

"Blind. Naive. Gullible. Take your pick." She hunched one shoulder. "None of them are exactly flattering."

"Brad was a master at pretending to be somebody he wasn't. That's why he was so good at his job." Nick grasped her chin and persuaded her to look at him. "It's no reflection on you that you didn't suspect anything."

"I was his wife!" she cried. "I knew him better

than anyone else in the world—or so I thought!'' Anguish lashed through her voice. "How could I not have figured out the truth?"

Nick shook her gently. "Don't blame yourself for what Brad did.''

"Why did he do it?" she pleaded. "Why did he lie to me?"

Nick hesitated. "Maybe he was afraid you wouldn't marry him if you knew what a dangerous job he had for a living.''

"He owed me the truth!"

"Yes. But maybe…he was too afraid of losing you.'' Nick had never examined Brad's actions in that light before. Probably because Nick himself had never met a woman worth the enormous effort of dividing his life in two. What a strain Brad must have lived under, always on guard not to let something slip, required to produce a constant stream of excuses to explain his comings and goings.

Now that Nick had met Juliet, however, he was beginning to understand how she might have been worth it to his brother.

Juliet made a sound that was half sniffle, half sigh. With a flick of her wrist she tugged off the rubber band holding back her ponytail, so that her pale gold hair spilled over her shoulders.

Nick's fingers itched to plunge through it. He deliberately scooted back his chair a few inches. It was reckless to sit so close to her, where the temptation to touch her was so strong.

This powerful attraction just didn't make sense. Juliet was utterly different from the women Nick usually went for. She was so damn…wholesome. Mom and apple pie. Peaches-and-cream complexion. Nick preferred his women a bit more down and dirty. A little on the wild side. Juliet's idea of a hot date was probably munching popcorn and holding hands at the movies.

Weird. Right now that actually sounded kind of fun to Nick.

Most of the women he encountered in his line of work had secret agendas of their own. He'd learned not to trust one word that fell from their pretty lips, even in the heat of passion. *Especially* in the heat of passion.

Juliet didn't possess one deceptive bone in her entire gorgeous body.

But deception, manipulation, looking out for number one—all were games Nick played very well. Games he enjoyed. And what game was more enjoyable than mutual seduction? As long as he and his partner both knew the score, where was the harm? So what if neither one of them was looking for a happily-ever-after. The physical pleasure they shared was no less real just because they were using each other.

It startled Nick to realize he could never use Juliet that way. No matter how high the stakes were.

He'd never come across a woman like her before, a woman so trusting and honest and gentle. A woman who combined vulnerability and strength in a way that made him simultaneously want to protect her and ravish her right here on the kitchen floor.

Cripes, get a grip! he scolded himself. This is Brad's wife you're lusting over, not some scheming adventuress who's been around the block a few times.

None of the women he'd known before had ever cried on Nick's shoulder.

Juliet sleeked her hair back from her face and imprisoned it in the rubber band again. She had long, elegant fingers and perfectly sculpted bone structure. Tears couldn't dim the hypnotic quality of those sapphire eyes. She'd make a great spy herself, Nick reflected. Foreign agents would probably trip all over themselves in their eagerness to reveal their secrets.

"I'm going to have some tea." Her voice was still a little hoarse from crying. "Would you like some?"

"Sure."

Juliet didn't actually want tea. The idea of putting anything into her stomach right now made her slightly queasy. But she needed an excuse to move away from Nick, some activity to hide her humiliation.

She couldn't believe she'd cried in his arms.

Worse, that she'd found a measure of comfort there. Which made no sense at all. Nick was the one who'd caused her this terrible pain, who'd taken a wrecking ball to her marriage. She should have kicked him out of her house, and instead she'd wound up blubbering into the front of his pullover sweater.

Of course, in all fairness, Nick wasn't the person who'd lied to her.

Juliet stared blankly into the open cupboard. Now, what had she been about to—? Tea, that was it. She pulled boxes onto the counter. Chamomile, orange spice, cinnamon apple... "What kind would you like?" she asked over her shoulder.

"Uh...just the regular kind."

She grabbed a box of English breakfast. "Coming right up." She filled the kettle, plunked it onto the stove. Now there would be a long, awkward silence while they waited for the water to boil.

How could Brad have betrayed her like this?

Her face must have conveyed her thoughts. Nick

came over and put his hands on her shoulders. Heat radiated down her arms, spread up her neck in a flush. Such big, strong, competent hands he had. Hands that were capable of such tenderness and, apparently, such violence. Juliet shuddered.

"Hey," he said gruffly. "I'm sorry. I didn't know all the trouble I was going to cause by looking for you. If I could do it all over again, I wouldn't have tried to find you."

Juliet managed to choke out a bitter laugh. "But then Emma and I might have been run over."

"Well...there is that."

She watched his square chin jut out in rueful acknowledgment. She refused to glance any higher than that. She couldn't bear to see the pity in his eyes. Or perhaps a glimmer of the contempt he must feel toward her for being such a sucker.

Besides, Nick's eyes unnerved Juliet for some reason. There was that eerie resemblance to Brad's, of course. But there was also something unique and mysterious in them that compelled her to look deeper, as if to catch a glimpse of Nick's soul.

Objectively speaking, she could hardly deny that Nick was a very good-looking man. What had the motel clerk called him? A stud. Six feet two inches of pure, unabashed masculinity. With that jet-black hair, those sexy gray eyes, that rugged, granite-jawed face, he was every woman's secret fantasy come to life.

But this—this pull, this bond, this...attraction Juliet felt seemed to run deeper than a normal female response to Nick's impressive physical attributes. And that was something else about him that puzzled and disturbed her.

There was more Juliet needed to ask him. About Brad. About Brad's other life. About his death. But her emotional equilibrium teetered on a precarious perch right now. The answers Nick gave her might send her screaming over the edge.

As if to mimic Juliet's state of mind, the kettle began to shriek. She turned to pour boiling water over the tea bags in their cups.

"What are you making, Mommy?"

She nearly scalded herself at the sound of Emma's voice from the doorway. "Just some tea. Want some?"

"With cream and sugar?"

"With honey and skim milk."

Emma rocked back and forth on her heels. "Gramma always gives me cream and sugar."

"Gramma spoils you."

"She says that's what grammas are for."

Despite the storm of turmoil inside her, Juliet couldn't help but smile. "I guess she's right about that." She got another cup from the cupboard. Then she pounced on Emma, tickling her mercilessly between the ribs. "And mommies are for being big and mean and grouchy!"

"Stop!" Emma squealed with delight.

No matter what else Brad had done, he'd given Juliet the most precious gift of her life. As long as she had Emma, she could survive anything.

Chapter 5

Nick hated being cooped up, even when the temperature outside was flirting with zero. Rather than return to his motel after leaving Juliet's, he drove downtown and walked around for a while. Motion had always helped him think anyway.

He felt lousy about what he'd done to her. And in a way, hadn't he betrayed his own brother, too? Yet Brad must have expected the truth to come out, when he set things up so Nick would go looking for Juliet. Knowing how devastated she would be, Brad must have had a pretty powerful reason for Nick to find her.

Emma?

Juliet would have been a few months pregnant when Brad died. Far enough along so that Brad would have known he was going to be a father. Had he meant for Nick to step in for him, to be a substitute father for his child, if Brad never came back from that last, disastrous mission?

If so, he'd picked a poor stand-in. Nick, a father? He wasn't even sure he knew how to be an uncle, for Pete's sake. Sure, Emma was a cute kid. Maybe Nick was even starting to feel something for her besides curiosity. But he didn't know the first thing about being a parent. God knows, he and Brad had certainly never had much in the way of role models.

Weren't fathers supposed to be there to tuck you in bed at night, to teach you how to ride a bike, to applaud your performance in the school play? How could Nick do any of those things from halfway around the world, from whatever trouble spot he was assigned to next?

Besides, Juliet would have to approve his role as father figure. Right now, that seemed about as likely as a tropical heat wave hitting Lake Andrew in time for Christmas.

Nick had forgotten to wear his cap, so the threat of frostbite to his ears finally drove him back to his car. He wove his way through strolling holiday shoppers, past small clumps of carolers gathered on street corners. School kids, mostly. He pictured Emma someday, bundled up against the cold, singing her heart out.

In the distance, church bells chimed the hour. Sunlight sparkled off mounds of snow pushed against the curbs by city snowplows. Christmas decorations bobbed overhead from long wires strung across the streets. Everyone Nick encountered seemed to be smiling. Was it just the season, or was everyone in this town always so friendly? He'd lost count of the number of times complete strangers had said hello to him.

He was way out of his element here in the heartland. He should do Juliet a favor and just go back to Washington. But it nagged at Nick's conscience, the way he'd stormed into her life like a tornado, shattered her treasured memories, destroyed her peaceful existence. How could he just blow out of town right away and leave her to cope with the wreckage alone?

Besides, he'd made a promise to Emma while the three of them had been drinking tea in Juliet's kitchen earlier today.

"If you're my uncle, am I s'posed to call you Uncle Nick?" Emma had asked.

An odd warmth had seeped through Nick's chest. "Sure," he replied, sneaking a glance in Juliet's direction. "I'd like that." Juliet's face stayed carefully noncommittal.

Emma kicked her legs back and forth and blew energetically on her tea. "Then, Uncle Nick, will you help me build a snowman?"

He peered out the window into the yard. A few patches of dried grass showed through in places. "Not much snow left out there. I think we'll have to wait till it snows again."

"*Then* can we build a snowman?"

"Yep."

"Promise?"

"I promise."

Emma had beamed with delight. Juliet hadn't.

Nick wasn't in the habit of making promises, but this minor one had seemed safe enough. And now that he'd given his word, of course, he had no choice but to keep it.

He drove back to his motel. There was a rack of newspapers outside the office. He bought one and checked the forecast. Snow wasn't predicted for two more days.

A dream. That's what this whole improbable scene felt like. She had phoned Nick with the intention of meeting him for coffee—and questions. But he'd insisted on treating her to dinner at the ritziest restaurant in town. And here she was, Juliet Ryan, single mom and mild-mannered librarian, dining on prime rib at the famous Lakeshore House, rubbing elbows with the elite, sharing a candlelit table with the most gorgeous man in the restaurant.

Who also happened to be a spy.

"Are you, um, between assignments now?" Was that the proper terminology? She wasn't a big James Bond fan.

Other questions swarmed through Juliet's mind. Questions about Brad that only Nick could answer. But as their meal progressed, her determination to ask them faltered. How could she demand the details of her husband's death in this sedate, elegant setting?

"Between assignments." A grimace flickered across Nick's face like a passing shadow. "Yeah. You could call it that."

"What would *you* call it?"

He didn't answer right away, as if cutting a piece of roast beef required all his concentration. He set down his knife. "Officially I'm on a three-month leave of absence."

"And...when does that end?"

Wry humor tilted one edge of his mouth. "Translation—how soon will I go away and leave you alone?"

"No, of course not!" Heat flowed to Juliet's cheeks. "Well…" She toyed with the food on her plate. "Maybe."

"I have to be back in Washington January 2."

"Oh." Barely two weeks away. "Do you…have plans for the holidays?"

"Nope." Nick chuckled. "Don't look so panic-stricken. I'm not going to horn in on yours."

Politeness demanded she say it. "You're more than welcome to—"

"No, I'm not." He leaned over the silk damask tablecloth. The candlelight threw his chiseled features into even bolder relief. "You can hardly wait for me to leave town, so you can start going about the business of forgetting I exist."

Juliet dropped her knife with a *clink*. "I doubt I'll be very successful at *that*."

Nick's mouth twitched. "From most women, I'd take that as a compliment."

"I'm sure most of them mean it that way."

He grinned. Juliet was startled by the primitive current of desire that switched on inside her. "Thanks," he said. "I think."

She busied herself with eating, confused by the strange electricity that had charged the air between them. For a few minutes the only sounds were the soft strains of the string trio in the corner, the tinkling of silverware and crystal, the muted murmur of conversation at other tables.

Nick poured more wine into her glass. "Back to our original subject. The holidays."

"My whole family gathers for Christmas dinner at

my parents' house.'' Juliet took a reckless sip of wine. Normally, one glass was her limit. ''You're invited, of course. If you're still in town then.''

Nick swirled the contents of his glass and studied them with dark contemplation. ''I doubt your family would welcome me with open arms, considering the way I've hurt you.''

''Heavens, I'm not going to tell them the truth about Brad!'' Until the exclamation passed her lips, Juliet hadn't given the matter conscious thought.

Nick set down his glass and frowned. ''Why not?''

''Because my family adored Brad.'' Now that she'd made her decision, Juliet knew it was the right one. ''What purpose would it serve to disillusion them, too?''

Nick had to admit, she had a point. He tightened his fingers around his glass, visualized snapping the stem in two. ''So you're going to let them go on believing my brother was the salt of the earth, huh?'' Well, well, well. Could that actually be jealousy he heard in his voice?

A spark of indignation caught fire in Juliet's eyes. ''Brad was a fine man! He was a wonderful...'' The light in her eyes dimmed as her words trailed off. Plainly it had struck her all over again, how badly she'd been deceived.

The way she'd automatically rushed to Brad's defense sharpened that small sting of jealousy. Nick certainly had to give her credit for loyalty. But the pain that shimmered across her beautiful face made him want to crawl under the table with guilt.

''Brad was part of our family,'' Juliet continued with quiet dignity. ''It would be petty of me to destroy their love for his memory with the truth.''

Nick tried not to wince. "The way I did to you."

Juliet traced the rim of her glass with her finger. "You didn't intend to hurt me." She sighed. "But once I saw you, once I found out you were Brad's brother, you didn't have much choice."

"That's a generous interpretation." *Damn it, Brad, did you appreciate how lucky you were to have this woman?*

Juliet shook her head. "It's the truth, that's all." She pushed her glass away. "Do I wish I could have gone on in blissful ignorance, believing my husband was something he wasn't?" She rubbed her temple. "No. Maybe. I don't know. Right now I'm just so confused...."

Nick reached across the table and covered her hand with his. He wasn't sure why he did it exactly. He could hardly expect her to derive any comfort from *his* touch. But somehow the gesture felt...natural.

Juliet offered him a faint smile. Tonight she was wearing her hair the way he liked it, long and loose and flowing over her shoulders. "Anyway, the invitation to Christmas dinner still stands."

"I don't want to intrude."

"Sharing Christmas isn't an intrusion."

"Isn't it?" He grazed his thumb over her knuckles. "I wouldn't know. Christmas was practically an alien concept while Brad and I were growing up."

"It was?" That delectable space between her eyebrows puckered. "Don't tell me Brad lied to me about his religion, too."

Nick shook his head. "It's just that our parents weren't big on celebrating the holiday. Any holiday. They considered it all a bunch of useless sentimental claptrap." When she started to tug her hand away, he held on tighter. "Hey, don't look at *me*. That's a direct quote from my father." Nick swallowed some wine. It tasted bitter all of a sudden.

Juliet's disapproval changed to a blend of surprise and sympathy. "How sad! Not that I have any right to criticize your parents, but I think they cheated you out of something really important."

Their parents had cheated Nick and Brad out of plenty that was important. Christmas came way down on the list. But Nick wasn't about to get all touchy-feely and share the emotional deprivations of his childhood with her.

To divert her from that direction, he deliberately provoked her. "You have to admit, Christmas is pretty commercial." He shrugged. "Isn't the real underlying purpose to boost the economy by pumping up retail sales?"

"No!" Juliet seemed horrified by the suggestion. "I agree, Christmas can get too commercialized, but it means much more than just buying presents for people."

"Don't you buy presents for your family?"

"Sure I do! But that isn't what makes it Christmas." A wistful tenderness softened her features. "Christmas is all about love and family and traditions. About peace on earth, goodwill toward—" She broke off at the skeptical slant of Nick's brow. A rueful smile tipped her luscious mouth. "All right, it's corny. But it's true. Christmas means... It means magic and miracles." She reached over and touched his cheek. Exasperation mingled with sadness. "Nick Ryan, didn't you ever believe in Santa Claus?"

Never. And he'd witnessed far too much suffering in his life to believe in miracles.

But whether or not he wanted to believe it, Nick was starting to feel something for Juliet that ran deeper than guilt or sympathy or good old-fashioned lust.

Something that surprised him even more than magic.

"Do you really think she'll like it?" Nick peered dubiously into the shopping bag for the third time since they'd left the toy store. After dinner, he'd asked Juliet to help him buy a Christmas present for Emma. Although she'd teased him about contributing to the "commercialization" of the holiday, she'd been touched by his request and agreed to accompany him to the mall.

"She'll love it," Juliet assured him again. "Even if it's not a real live puppy."

He pulled the floppy-eared stuffed animal from the bag and regarded it nose to nose for a moment. "Okay. You're the expert."

Juliet found his anxiety rather endearing. "I guarantee, Emma will sleep with it every night."

"Yeah?" Nick carefully placed the toy dog back into the bag. "I hope so. I'd like to give her something she could sort of…remember me by."

Juliet lowered her eyes to her steaming coffee mug. Why should it bother her, that Nick would be going away soon, that she and Emma might never see him again?

They were drinking coffee in the window of a gourmet coffee outlet inside the mall. The stores would be closing soon, and people bustled by in a hurry, loaded down with shopping bags and determined looks on their faces. The coffee place itself was deserted except for the clerk behind the counter.

Juliet had lost her nerve at dinner, hadn't asked Nick any of the questions that were the whole point of going out with him tonight. This could be her last chance. For all she knew, he might pick up and leave town tomorrow.

Now or never.

She eased into the emotional minefield with a relatively simple question. "Nick, why didn't Brad tell anyone he was married? That man I spoke to at the CIA…"

"Don Mason."

Juliet nodded. "He told me the CIA didn't know Brad had a wife until after he died."

"That's right." Nick stretched out his long legs from beneath the small wrought-iron table they were sitting at. "Brad never informed the Agency he was married."

"Why not?" Juliet's fingers curled into fists. "I mean, I can see why he wanted to keep his job a secret from me. It was unforgivable, but understandable."

Nick probed his cheek with his tongue, as if searching for words to defend his brother. But there was no justifying what Brad had done.

Juliet didn't wait for Nick to try. "What reason could Brad have had for not telling the Agency he was married? If he had, then at least I would have been notified right away when he was killed."

"How did you find out?" Nick asked quietly.

A chill shuddered down Juliet's spine. "When Brad didn't come back from his trip the day he was supposed to, I got worried." Worried? Frantic was more like it. She didn't think she could live through another agonizing week like that again. Ever. "At first I tried to tell myself he'd just been delayed. Travel connections can be unreliable in some parts of the world. Maybe he was stranded someplace where he couldn't get to a phone to call me."

Juliet plucked little pieces off her napkin. "Finally I called the State Department. I figured they would be the logical ones to help locate an American citizen missing overseas." Her fingers moved faster. "They said they would do what they could. Several days later an official called me back."

She drew in a harsh breath and forced her hands into stillness. "He said he was sorry to have to inform me that Brad had died in a plane crash off the coast of Africa." She blinked back tears. "The wreckage was never located. Except now I know there *wasn't* any wreckage."

"I'm sorry." Nick put his hand over hers. The gesture was becoming familiar, even though she'd only known him for...what? A couple of days? The touch of his hand was nice, made her feel sort of warm and tingly all over.

But Juliet didn't want to get used to that feeling. She didn't want to depend on that strong, comforting hand being there for her. After discovering what Brad had done, she wasn't going to depend on any man ever again.

She slipped her fingers from beneath Nick's on the pretense of sipping coffee. "Anyway, I still don't understand why Brad would have kept our marriage a secret from the Agency." She kept both hands safely wrapped around her mug.

Nick leveled a steady gaze at her. Those impenetrable gray eyes were about as revealing as chips of granite. "Brad might have been worried that marriage could hurt his career."

Juliet frowned. "How?"

Nick glanced over his shoulder before replying, as if about to reveal a state secret. "It's not official Agency policy, but Don Mason, Brad's superior, does tend to delegate the most dangerous, important, career-building assignments to agents who are single."

"Why?"

"No wife or children, no divided loyalties, no distractions." Nick spread his hands. "An agent sometimes has to make split-second, life-or-death decisions. Decisions that might be affected by the thought of loved ones back home."

"Let me get this straight." Anger began to simmer in the pit of Juliet's stomach. "You're saying Brad chose to hide my existence so he could go on risking his life?"

Nick's jaw shifted to an obstinate angle. "I'm sure he wanted to keep doing his job. It was important work, and he was good at it. He didn't want to wind up stuck behind some desk."

"Oh, mercy me, a desk job." Juliet covered her mouth in mock horror. "You make it sound like a death sentence."

Irritation glinted in Nick's eyes. "More like a prison term, for a man like Brad."

"And for a man like you, I suppose?" Why should she care if Nick wanted to risk his life, get himself killed, all for some macho idea of adventure? But she did care. And that made her even more furious. "How could Brad have chosen his work over me? Over our unborn child?'' Juliet slammed her palms to the table. ''How?''

Nick pushed his face close to hers. ''Because he was raised to believe career comes before family, that's why.'' Immediately he drew back, as if regretting that revelation. A shutter dropped over his features.

But Juliet wasn't about to let that intriguing statement pass. ''What do you mean? Are you talking about your parents?''

Nick aimed his glance out the window at the bustling parade of shoppers. ''Let's just say their children weren't their highest priority.''

''Their careers were?''

He cocked his thumb at her. ''Bingo.''

Juliet's anger subsided. ''How sad. For you and Brad, I mean.''

''Yeah, well…'' Nick rolled his shoulders as if to shrug off her sympathy. ''We survived.''

No doubt he chose to ignore the pain that lay buried deep beneath those two words. But Juliet could hear it. ''Your mother was an archaeologist, is that what you said?''

''Both she and my father were. Highly respected ones. Top authorities in their field.'' Nick dusted his knuckles against his jaw. ''But it's a very competitive field. You can't rest on your laurels. You've got to keep striving, coming up with new, exciting discoveries to keep your name in the academic journals, or the research grants dry up. People forget who you are.''

''So your parents were too busy to give you and Brad the attention you deserved.''

''At least we had each other.''

"You must have been very close."

Nick's gaze slid to one side. Obviously he wasn't comfortable discussing relationships. "I suppose."

"But then—" Juliet pinched the bridge of her nose, trying to make sense of this. "Why didn't Brad at least tell *you* about our marriage?"

"I don't know." From the way Nick started fidgeting, Juliet could tell she'd hit a sore spot. So Nick had wondered that himself. "In our line of work," he said with a shrug, "secrecy becomes second nature."

"I can't imagine keeping a secret like that from my brother."

"No. You wouldn't." He picked up the shopping bag and stood. "You done with your coffee? Looks like this place is about to close."

Juliet happened to know they wouldn't be closing for another half hour, but she didn't argue. She also didn't ask the next question on her list—why had Brad arranged it so Nick could find her? She preferred to believe it was because Brad had meant for Nick to look after her and Emma if he should die in the line of duty.

But the awful way Brad had deceived her made Juliet wonder whether his intentions had truly been that noble.

"Nick." They were crossing the parking lot, nearly to his car when Juliet hooked his arm and drew him to a stop.

"What is it?" His dark brows drew together with concern.

"Yesterday, you said the State Department told me that Brad died in a plane crash in order to—to cover up the real circumstances of his death."

Nick moved closer, as if to shelter her from the

frigid wind. Or as if to protect her from what she was about to ask.

Juliet's teeth chattered, but not from the cold. "If Brad wasn't killed in a plane crash, then how did he really die?"

Chapter 6

Maybe Juliet didn't need a drink for this conversation, but Nick sure as hell did. He pulled into the first bar they passed on the way back to her place.

"What would you like?" he asked her. She studied the neon beer signs, the bottles of liquor lined up in front of the mirror behind the well-worn bar. It didn't take a trained intelligence agent to conclude that she didn't hang out in saloons too often.

"A hot toddy?" she said uncertainly.

Nick bit back a grin. "Irish whiskey," he told the bartender.

"Coming right up."

Nick carried their drinks to a back booth. Most of the other patrons were perched on stools, eyes glued to the football game on the wide-screen TV behind the bar. The majority wore overalls and brimmed caps that sported feed company advertisements. Sawdust and peanut shells littered the floor, while the air was a miasma of stale beer, cigarette smoke and wet mittens. Not exactly the Rainbow Room, but the dim lighting and the background noise would at least give them a measure of privacy.

Nick slid into the booth and sat across from Juliet. He tossed back a healthy swallow before he started talking. "Okay. You want to know how Brad really died."

Juliet's drink sat untouched. She hunched forward as if braced for a blow, hands knotted in her lap. They had the thermostat cranked way up in here, but she hadn't taken off her coat yet. Maybe she was planning to leap up and flee into the night as soon as she heard the answer to her question.

Her eyes were dark hollows in the murky light. "If Brad didn't die in a plane crash…"

"He was killed trying to capture a terrorist who'd murdered dozens of innocent people."

Juliet lifted her glass and downed a hefty gulp. She stared steadily at Nick the whole time. Without even blinking. She set down her drink with an abrupt jerk of her wrist.

"The U.S. government had been after this bastard for years." Nick wasn't even sure if what he said was registering. Juliet still wore a shell-shocked stare. "Three years ago, the Agency got a tip that he was living under a fake identity in a country considered to be one of our allies."

Her lips finally moved. "What country?"

Nick was relieved when she finally spoke, even though the information she wanted was classified. "I'm not at liberty to say. But the Agency's analysis was that their national security forces weren't up to the job of nabbing this guy."

Juliet's eyes came back to life, darting rapidly back and forth as if trying to grasp the entire picture at once. "So the CIA sent in someone to do the job."

"Yes."

"Brad."

"Along with several others."

Juliet bowed her head and shaded her eyes with her hand. "I can't believe this."

"They were a team, with orders to snatch the terrorist and hustle him back to the U.S. to stand trial—"

Juliet snapped up her head. "We can't possibly be talking about my husband!" A cloud of anguished disbelief filled her beautiful blue eyes. "Brad never displayed the slightest inclination toward violence. He—he didn't even like to watch football, for heaven's sake!" She waved at the TV screen, then let her hand fall helplessly to the table. "I can't believe we're talking about the same person," she murmured.

Nick knew exactly how she felt. He'd been seized by the same disorienting grip of unreality the moment he'd found proof of Brad's marriage.

"I just can't picture Brad as—as some kind of Rambo." Juliet drank some more of her toddy. Nick doubted she even tasted it. "Tell me what happened."

"Something went wrong." Nick dragged a hand over his face. "The local authorities showed up just when Brad's team made their move against the terrorist. Maybe they got tipped off by the same source, or maybe the whole fiasco was some kind of setup. Either way, everyone started shooting." Nick swallowed some whiskey. "In all the confusion, Brad got killed in the cross fire."

Juliet brought a shaky hand to her mouth. She made

a faint, muffled sound, her eyes huge with shock and sorrow.

There was nothing Nick could do for her except finish the story. "The surviving members of Brad's team managed to smuggle his body out of the country. They had to keep the location of his death a secret, you see. It would have damaged relations between our two governments if the other nation found out we'd been operating inside their borders."

Juliet lowered her hand. "What...happened to the terrorist?" she whispered.

Nick's mouth tightened with grim satisfaction. "When all the dust settled, our guys wound up with him. He was tried and convicted a year ago. He'll be spending the rest of his life in an American prison cell."

"But didn't the other country learn where he was captured, when he went on trial?"

"By that time, the details of how he got to the U.S. had been so muddied that the other government had no proof to back up their suspicions." Nick finished his drink. "That's why it was essential to hide the location and true circumstances of Brad's death."

"So when I called the State Department to report my husband missing..."

"Once they put two and two together and figured out who Brad really was, the State Department obviously agreed to cooperate with the CIA and tell you a phony story. Since it was a matter of national security." Nick slid out of the booth. "You want another drink?"

"No. Thank you."

He left her studying the chipped fake wood grain in the tabletop. By the time he returned, some of the color had come back into her face. Either that, or she was getting overheated with that coat on.

"What Brad was sent to do was illegal, wasn't it?" Juliet barely waited for Nick to sit down again. "Operating inside another country without that government's permission. Aren't there laws against that?"

Nick took time to thumb a smudge from his glass before replying. "This particular terrorist was wanted for blowing up an American embassy."

"I've no doubt he committed horrible crimes, but—"

"Part of the embassy contained a day-care center for employees' children."

Juliet went silent, a sick film of horror sliding over her expression.

"Of the thirty-one people killed in the blast, over half were children."

Her lips parted on a sound of anguish. "Dear God."

"So you see, sometimes, justice requires bending the rules a little." And sometimes, bending them a lot.

Juliet gazed past Nick's shoulder. An observer might assume she was trying to glimpse the progress of the football game. Nick knew better. When she looked at him again, her eyes were shiny with tears.

"I'm sorry for what happened to those people. To those—" she fought to get the word out "—children." She brushed her fingertips over her eyes. "But that doesn't justify breaking the law. Violating another nation's sovereignty."

Nick struggled to subdue his rising temper. "I think it does."

"Laws have to apply to everyone, or they're meaningless."

"Are you saying Brad deserved to die?"

Crimson flooded her cheeks. "Don't be ridiculous!" she exclaimed. "But I do believe it was wrong, what he was doing. It was wrong for the Agency to send him there, and it was wrong for the Agency to cover up the facts of his death."

"There was a greater good at stake—"

Juliet flung out her hand. "I don't care about some abstract principle you can twist around to justify doing anything you want to. I'm talking about human beings." She clamped her fist to her heart. "Me, for one. Losing my husband, being lied to by my own government..."

"There was a reason for—"

"And Emma, having to grow up without a father, all because Brad was someplace he shouldn't have been, doing something he should never have been sent to do."

"He was doing his job. He gave his life for a good—"

"And you!" Juliet cried. "You lost your own brother! How could you allow his death to become part of a government conspiracy to hide the truth?"

Nick answered through clenched teeth. "It was my duty."

"Your duty. Your job. I'm sick of hearing those words." She tossed a swatch of golden hair over her shoulder. "What about your *family*, Nick?"

With controlled movements he lifted his glass and set it down, over and over, leaving interlocking rings of moisture on the table. "What would exposing the truth have accomplished, other than stirring up friction with another country?'' Nick grimaced. ''It wouldn't have brought my brother back.''

''What if it could have?'' Juliet planted her elbows on the table and aimed a judgmental stare at him. ''Would you still have chosen your precious duty over your brother's life?''

''No. Of course not.'' Nick clutched his glass nearly hard enough to shatter it.

''Well.'' Juliet relaxed backward and nodded slowly. ''That's something, anyway.''

''It's getting late. You probably need to pick up Emma—''

''Just one more thing.'' She pinned her hand over his wrist to restrain him from leaving. ''You didn't know Brad had a wife until you tracked me here to Lake Andrew, is that right?''

''Yes.'' Her fingers were soft and smooth, warm velvet against Nick's skin. So why did they remind him of handcuffs?

''Yet the Agency learned I was Brad's wife right after he died.''

Nick saw where she was headed. He'd already been down this road himself.

Juliet increased the pressure on his wrist. ''So the Agency hid the truth from *you*, too. By not informing you Brad was married.''

''Maybe they assumed I already knew it.''

''Or maybe they were more concerned about covering up their illegal actions than telling you something important about your own brother.''

''Sometimes...personal considerations have to take a back seat.''

''A back seat to what? National security? Our marriage was hardly a threat to world peace.''

Nick didn't argue with her. Truth was, it rankled him, too, that the Agency higher-ups hadn't passed on the fact of Juliet's existence to him.

Her lips curved with distaste. "How can you stand all the secrecy, all the lies?" She released his wrist as if it had burned her. "How can you live your life with every move you make calculated to deceive someone?"

Juliet wouldn't understand. She lived in a sheltered, innocent world where people were polite and followed the rules and believed that good always triumphed over evil.

From Nick's perspective, they might as well believe in Santa Claus.

Despite Juliet's protests, Nick insisted they stop by her parents' house to pick up Emma on the way home.

"It's getting late, Nick. She's probably fallen asleep already. I can wait and pick her up in the morning."

"It's not far out of the way. I'd hate for you to have to make a special trip over there."

Juliet wasn't sure whether Nick's real motivation was to meet her parents or to see Emma again, but she did know it was useless to argue. Especially when he had control of the steering wheel.

She rang her parents' doorbell. The porch light came on just before a nearby curtain flicked aside. "Goodness, it's you," her mother exclaimed when she opened the door. "You always go around to the back, so I thought it must be—oh, my land!" She clapped a hand to her heart when she got her first good look at Nick. "Why, I can hardly believe it!"

She lowered her glasses to goggle at him. "Juliet told us you looked like Brad, but my heavens, you're practically the spitting image!"

Juliet was thankful that earlier today she'd broken the news to her parents that Brad had a brother who'd shown up out of the blue. But her mother still stared as if she'd seen a ghost. "Dear me, where are my manners?" she said. "Please, come in. Come in!"

Juliet stepped inside ahead of Nick. "Emma's not still awake, is she?"

"Oh, you know I never have the heart to make her go to bed this early."

"*Early?* Mom, it's—"

"Carl? Carl! Come see who's here," her mother called as she shut the door behind them. "It's Brad's brother!"

"Mom, I'd like you to meet Nick Ryan. Nick, this is—"

"What a special treat!" Dora Hansen enfolded Nick in a warm, welcoming bear hug. Not an easy task, considering he was over six feet tall and she was barely five-two.

Juliet couldn't help smiling at Nick's stunned expression. After a moment's pause, he circled his arms around her mother in a fair imitation of a hug.

When Dora drew back, her eyes were moist. "I can't tell you how wonderful it is to meet Brad's brother." She kept patting Nick's arm as if testing him for freshness. "He was a dear, dear boy, and we all miss him so much."

"Er, thank you." Nick wore the look of a man who's suddenly gotten in way over his head. Was he starting to sweat?

Just then Juliet's father hustled into the entryway

carrying a newspaper folded open to the crossword puzzle. "What's all the ruckus—well, for gosh sakes!" He pulled up short, chin dropping to his chest.

"Pop, this is Nick Ryan, Brad's brother."

"I should say that's obvious!" Carl Hansen dropped a distracted kiss on top of her head. "Hello, sweetie." He seized Nick's hand and pumped it with gusto. "How do you do, young man?"

A comma of black hair shook loose over Nick's forehead. "Fine, sir. And you?"

"Doesn't he look just like our Brad?" Dora pressed her hands to her cheeks and gazed at Nick with rapturous wonder.

Carl shook his balding head in amazement. "Yep, yep…he sure does."

Emma skipped out of the living room, dragging a Raggedy Ann doll by the foot. "Hi, Mommy!" She flung herself against Juliet's legs, then peered shyly around them. "Hi, Uncle Nick."

"Hey, Emma." He winked at her.

Emma giggled.

Juliet's parents exchanged a pleased *Aha!* sort of look that set warning bells clanging inside her head.

"What are we all standing in the entry for, anyway?" Her father rubbed his hands vigorously together. "It's cold in here. Let's go into the living room and—"

"We should go, Pop." Juliet intended to nip this in the bud right away. "It's way past Emma's bedtime."

"Aw, Mommy…"

"But you just got here!" Dora protested. "And we're so looking forward to getting to know Nick.…"

Her eyes gleamed with a sneaky maternal glow Juliet recognized all too well. Dora clapped her hands. "I've got an idea!"

"What's that, dear?" Her father, the perfect straight man for her mother. Juliet rolled her eyes and prepared herself.

"Tomorrow's the day we're all going to pick out the tree, remember?" Dora trained a benevolent look on Nick like a spotlight. "It's sort of a family tradition, you see. Every year we all pile into the car and drive out to Lundberg's Tree Farm—"

"Actually, now it takes *two* cars," Juliet's father interrupted with an aside to Nick.

"And we choose a tree together! Then we cut it down and bring it back here and have a party while we decorate it. I bake cookies—"

"I wanna help!" Emma jiggled on her toes.

"Emma helps me bake cookies, and we have hot apple cider and sing Christmas carols, and Carl gets out his old violin—"

"Mom, I think Nick probably—"

"Gosh, I'd love to," he said. "Thank you for inviting me, Mrs. Hansen."

If Juliet's mother had beamed any brighter, the whole house would have blown a fuse. She linked her arm through Nick's and patted his sleeve. "Please. Call me Dora."

"Yay! Uncle Nick's coming tomorrow!" Emma threw her arms around Juliet's knees and hugged so hard, she nearly tipped her mother over.

Juliet resigned herself to the inevitable after scanning the faces crowded into the entryway. Her delighted parents, one on either side of Nick, as thrilled as if their prodigal son had returned home. Emma, bouncing with glee, no doubt looking forward to showing off her newfound uncle to her cousins.

And Nick, towering above the others, bewildered but pleased by all the attention. Those heartstopping gray eyes met Juliet's, trapped her gaze, made her forget to breathe for a minute.

He wasn't Brad. Despite the physical similarities in their rugged build and handsome features, Juliet had no trouble keeping them separate. For one thing, although she'd loved Brad, she didn't recall his having quite the same powerful, disconcerting effect on her as Nick.

Sometimes she caught Nick watching her, not as if he were undressing her with his eyes, but as if he were making love to her.

Heat coiled inside her abdomen, a tight spring aching to explode. Nick was wrong for her, she knew that. She was never going to risk her heart on any man again. Especially a man who thrived on danger.

But whenever Juliet was near him, every cell in her body came alive.

"What time should I be here tomorrow?" Nick asked her mother. His gaze, though, kept holding Juliet's. Hypnotizing her. Caressing her. Seducing her.

Now *she* was the one starting to sweat.

Nick had never been on a hayride in his entire life. Until today. Another first to add to his list, along with chopping down a Christmas tree. Eating home-baked cookies. Singing Christmas carols, for Pete's sake!

He felt like a lost explorer who'd stumbled into the village of some previously unknown tribe and their exotic rituals.

Yet the Hansens had welcomed him like one of

their own. Juliet's brother, Tim, was blond, jovial and barrel-chested, an accountant who looked more like a farmer. He'd met Nick's gaze head-on and gripped his hand a little harder, a little longer than necessary when they'd first been introduced. A subtle warning that while the natives were friendly, they were fiercely protective of each other.

Better not mess around with my little sister's feelings was the clear message Tim's handshake had conveyed.

Tim's wife, Suzanne, had stood up on tiptoe to kiss Nick's cheek. "I feel like I know you already," she told him. "You look so much like your brother." Suzanne was petite and packed with energy. She needed it, chasing around after her four kids, her curly chestnut hair flying behind her.

The kids ranged in age from five to twelve years old. Kyle, Karly, Kristi and Kurt. Nick couldn't, for the life of him, keep straight which was which.

Late in the afternoon, in Dora's kitchen, he sought refuge from the tree-trimming party. The room smelled like apples and cinnamon. The door closed behind him, temporarily muting the chaos in the rest of the house. Kids racing up and down stairs, adults laughing, some good-natured squabbling over the exact placement of this or that ornament on the huge Norway spruce they'd lugged home. Someone—one of the younger kids, by the sound of it—was banging away on the old upright piano.

Nick was examining the display of children's artwork attached by magnets to the refrigerator when the noise from the living room swelled briefly, then faded.

"Oh!" Juliet pulled up short when she spotted him.

"I didn't know you were out here." Her cheeks turned as rosy as they'd been during the hayride out at the Christmas tree farm. "What are you doing? Hiding?" Her eyes twinkled like moonlight on snow.

"Shh." Nick raised a finger to his lips. "Don't tell anyone."

"Coward."

"I'm afraid your mother might try to stuff another ginger cookie down my throat if she catches me."

"Guess you don't need to worry about dinner tonight, huh?" She carried her empty crystal cup over to the stove and ladled in some hot cider. She wore a high-necked burgundy sweater and black slacks. She'd removed the wool-lined boots she'd worn on the tree-buying expedition, so her stocking feet made no sound when she crossed the floor. "By the way, I'm impressed," she said. "It's not everyone who can sing Christmas carols without actually knowing the words."

Nick stroked his chin sheepishly. "Didn't fool you, huh?"

She winked. "Don't worry. I don't think anyone else noticed."

He folded his arms and propped himself against the counter near the stove. "I like your family."

"They like you, too." Juliet blew on her cider and took a cautious sip. "You've made quite a hit with the kids. Especially Emma."

"She's a doll." Now, if only he could charm Emma's mother, too....

He wasn't sure why it mattered. Or why it pleased him to hear that Juliet's family liked him. In a few days he would be back in Washington, and after that he could be sent anywhere. He would probably never cross paths with any of them again.

"I can't get over how your relatives are willing to welcome a perfect stranger into their home." Nick still marveled at their warmth and openness. A far cry from the wariness, the distance, the suspicion that colored his interactions with most people.

"You're not a stranger." Above the rim of her cup, Juliet's pretty eyes were amused, faintly mocking. "You're family."

"No one's asked me what I do for a living."

"I told them you work for the government, but I didn't get too specific. Better have a cover story ready." Her lips puckered as if her cider had turned sour. "Then again, it's probably a snap for you to produce one on the spur of the moment. I imagine you've had lots of practice."

He let the subtle dig pass. "I feel like a rat, lying to them after they've been so nice to me."

"Don't let it bother you." She walked over to set her cup in the sink with a sharp chime of glass on cast iron. "After all, it didn't bother your brother."

"Juliet." Nick captured her arm when she walked past him. By reflex she resisted, then apparently decided not to waste energy arm wrestling with a stronger opponent. She lifted her chin and leveled a stony gaze at him.

"I'm sorry for the way Brad lied to you." Nick's low-pitched voice vibrated with intensity. "The way he lied to all of you." Her bones were slender, seeming fragile beneath the sleeve of her sweater. He sensed her muscles tensed against him, like a bird poised to take flight the instant he let go. "But I'm not Brad."

"No." She used her free hand to flick back a stray wisp of hair. "I would never make the mistake of thinking you were."

Had she decided Nick didn't measure up, after comparing the two of them?

He loosened his grip, not enough to let her escape quite yet. "Do you think it's fair to keep blaming me for what Brad did?"

"I don't blame you." But he saw the lie in her eyes, and knew that she blamed him for something.

He stroked his thumb across the soft underside of her arm, just below her elbow. "I never meant to hurt you."

"No." She licked her lips nervously, sending a shaft of heat to his loins. "I know you didn't."

Nick saw the change in her eyes, the exact moment when Juliet, too, recognized the electricity shimmering in the air. Man, but he wanted her! From the moment he'd laid eyes on her. Maybe even from the moment he'd first seen her face in that picture.

He knew it was impossible. Juliet represented a fantasy, a bunch of corny ideals that Nick had never even believed actually existed. Family. Honesty. Continuity and tradition. Warmhearted generosity that concealed no ulterior motives.

It would be selfish and unforgivable to take advantage of her, to indulge in that fantasy, to pretend that this mutual chemistry could ever lead anywhere.

He tugged her a few inches closer.

Juliet's eyes widened, twin blue lakes with turbulent currents swirling beneath the surface. Her fair skin was perfectly smooth, nearly translucent. As unflawed and untouchable as fine porcelain.

Nick raised a hand to touch her face.

Her cheek was warm. Soft. Tempting. He traced her exquisite bone structure with one finger, amazed by the high-voltage arousal that shot through him. Pleased by the quick hitch in her throat, by the way her breasts rose and fell a little faster.

"I want to kiss you," he said.

"I—" She sucked in a sharp breath. "I don't think that's such a good idea."

"Probably not."

"It…would just…complicate things even more."

"You're absolutely right." Nick brought his face close to hers. Juliet didn't shy away, just kept watching him with those huge, incredible eyes that filled his vision. "Does that mean you don't want me to kiss you?"

"I—I—" She gulped. Her breathing sped up even more. A tiny vein fluttered frantically in the pale column of her throat, just above the snug neck of her sweater. Her silky curtain of hair tickled the back of Nick's hand. She smelled wonderful close up, all sugar and spice, one hundred percent female.

Nick was willing to bet she would taste even better.

"I'm still waiting for an answer," he whispered into the delicious space between her lips. Her breath was warm, intoxicating, mingling with his. Nick wasn't going to be able to hold back much longer. If Juliet didn't give him a clear signal within the next second or two, then conscience be damned. He would have no choice but to haul off and—

The kitchen door banged open. Juliet flew backward as if launched from a cannon. Nick hastily arranged his elbow on the counter as if he'd been lounging there the whole time. Mr. Cool, Mr. Casual, that was him. Just like Bogart in *Casablanca*.

Unfortunately, Juliet's face was a dead giveaway. She was lit up like Rudolph's red nose.

Emma charged across the kitchen, dragging her grandmother behind her. "See, Gramma? We're almost out of cookies. We need to bake some more." She stretched up on tiptoe to show her the tray on top of the stove. "Oh, hi, Mommy. Uncle Nick, there you are! Me and Kristi have been looking for you to play hide-and-seek with us."

Dora took one glance at Nick and Juliet and immediately got the picture. "Oops!" She switched her focus with a discreet cough. "Emma, dear, let's go back into the living room. Nick can play with you girls later." The light in her eyes wasn't just a reflection off her glasses.

"But Gramma—"

"No, Mom, it's okay."

Now another child popped out from behind Dora's legs. Kristi, Nick guessed. "Gramma, I'm thirsty."

"Girls, come on. Let's go." Dora shooed them across the kitchen with a flap of her apron.

Then the two boys tumbled in, a tangle of pinwheeling arms and legs. "Gramma, Kyle won't let me play with the cow!"

"That cow belongs in the manger scene, Kurt. It isn't a toy. Kyle, stop teasing your little brother. All of you, go on, now! Into the living room. Honestly!" She finally herded them through the door.

As it swung shut, silence fell between Nick and Juliet with an awkward thud. What the heck was he supposed to do now? Nick wondered. Pick up where he'd left off? He was smooth, but he wasn't that smooth.

Juliet wasn't going to give him the chance anyway.

"I ought to help Mom and Suzanne with the kids," she mumbled. Still blushing to the roots of her long blond hair, she fled from the kitchen without meeting Nick's eyes.

He had to curb the impulse to chase after her.

Chapter 7

Juliet couldn't believe how close she'd come to kissing Nick. What was wrong with her anyway? She had every reason in the world for resenting him, yet there she'd stood, mooning at him like a lovesick schoolgirl. Terrified and thrilled with the anticipation of what he might do next. Ready to swoon into his arms and let him ravish her mouth with his.

After what Brad had done to her, Juliet was never going to let some handsome, smooth-talking hunk sweep her off her feet again. Especially not one who shared a gene pool with the man who'd betrayed her.

Thank heavens they'd been interrupted.

Her mother's mysterious, I've-got-a-secret smile had only added to Juliet's embarrassment for the rest of the afternoon. Once or twice she'd also caught Suzanne sidling her a speculative smile, which meant Mom had blabbed about the cozy little tableau she'd stumbled upon in the kitchen.

Nick, at least, had acted the perfect gentleman. He hadn't foisted any meaningful glances on Juliet, hadn't maneuvered to get her alone again, hadn't tried to cop a feel while they were gathered around the piano singing one final round of carols.

Of course, she reminded herself, Nick was a pro at acting like something he wasn't.

Another thing Juliet regretted was letting him drive her and Emma out to the tree farm earlier. Now he would have to drive them home, too, unless Tim and Suzanne would agree to strap two extra passengers onto the roof of their station wagon.

Briefly she considered it. At least she would escape being trapped in the intimate confines of Nick's car with him.

"Thanks again, Dora, Carl. I had a great time." Nick formally shook her parents' hands.

Juliet's mother naturally wasn't about to let him get away with that. She hugged him goodbye as if he were a soldier going off to war. "We're so glad you came, aren't we, Carl?"

"You betcha."

She patted Nick on the back a few more times before releasing him. "It's so nice for our Emma to have a new uncle." She flashed a transparent smile at Juliet. *So nice for our daughter to have a new man in her life.*

Except Juliet intended to push Nick *out* of her life as soon as possible.

"Is your coat buttoned up, Tinker Bell? Come on, let's go." She ushered Emma out the front door. "Goodbye, everyone."

A chorus of farewells trailed them down the steps. Nick lifted his hand. "Nice meeting all of you."

"I'm sure we'll be seeing you again soon," Dora sang across the yard.

As she settled into Nick's car, Juliet didn't dare look back at the house. She knew what she would see. Faces peeking out every window.

She only lived a couple miles away, but the drive seemed to take forever. Something had knocked her internal receptors out of whack so that her senses kept homing in on Nick. She registered everything about him in immediate, vivid detail—the sprinkling of dark hair on the backs of his hands as they relaxed expertly on the steering wheel...a whiff of the rum her father had slipped into the eggnog after all the kids had drunk their fill...the low vibration of his voice, thrumming along her nerve endings as he responded to Emma's chatter from the back seat.

Thank goodness for Emma. Juliet didn't think she could have held up her end of a conversation if her life depended on it. Her focus had gone completely haywire.

But there was no dodging the awkward moment after Nick walked them to the front door and stood waiting while Juliet unlocked it. Emma rushed inside. Now that the sun was down, the air had turned downright arctic.

Politeness demanded Juliet invite Nick in. Self-defense warned her not to. Even with Emma as chaperone, it was too hard to ignore the unwanted desires Nick aroused. The heat of his body reminded her how wonderful it had felt to stand close to him in her mother's kitchen, his hand caressing her face, his breath warming her lips. Juliet could still hear the seductive echo of him saying, "I want to kiss you."

Each time she looked into those sexy gray eyes, let

her gaze drop to his square jaw, his rugged, masculine mouth…Juliet craved him all over again. And she didn't want to stop with a kiss, either.

Which was exactly why she ought to tell him thanks for the ride, say goodbye and shut the door firmly in his face.

Instead, she said, "I'm going to fix a salad for supper, since we ate so many sweets this afternoon. Would you like to stay and have some?"

"Salad sounds good."

He was probably thinking it sounded like rabbit food. But maybe it sounded better than eating alone in a restaurant, or picking up fast food to take back to his empty motel room.

He followed Juliet inside and eased his broad shoulders out of his coat. "I could watch Emma for you, if that would help."

Juliet hesitated. It wasn't that she feared Nick might suddenly turn out to be a kidnapper, or start telling Emma stories about her father the spy. But the more time he spent with Emma, the more attached she was going to become to him. Already she'd begun to regard Nick with a starry-eyed case of hero worship that had Juliet a little worried.

She didn't want Emma to get hurt when Nick left town.

Did that give her the right, though, to prevent Emma from bonding with her own uncle?

"Thanks," Juliet told him. "I'm sure Emma would enjoy that. Hope you can stand another round of hide-and-seek."

Nick groaned, but he was grinning when he went off in search of Emma.

Juliet did her best to ignore the melting effect his

crooked smile had on her insides. Unfortunately, she was about as successful as a snowman ignoring the spring thaw.

"Must be my scintillating company," Nick said. "Emma fell asleep."

Juliet straightened from the dishwasher. Nick had volunteered to clean up after they'd finished eating, but she'd waved him away when Emma insisted on dragging him off to play some more.

Nick hadn't minded. He was still intrigued by the idea he had a niece, and got a kick out of observing the workings of a three-year-old mind.

Besides, Emma demanded his full attention, which allowed Nick to forget about his troublesome attraction to Juliet. At least for a while.

But now he was alone with her, for the first time since he'd come within a heartbeat of kissing her in her mother's kitchen.

"She fell asleep already?" Juliet flipped back a curtain of hair that had fallen forward while she was bent over the dishwasher. "Poor thing. All the excitement this afternoon must have tuckered her out."

"I put her on the bed, took off her shoes and covered her with a blanket," Nick said.

"You did?" Juliet lifted her eyebrows in surprise.

"Hope that was okay." He'd felt kind of clumsy at it. He'd never tucked a kid in bed before, and memories of his own childhood sure didn't offer much helpful information on how it was done.

At least he'd managed not to wake Emma up. Truth was, putting her to bed had given Nick a sense of…satisfaction. A kind of pride. Emma *was* his niece, after all. Why shouldn't he be proud, when it was obvious that she was smarter and cuter and had more personality than any other kid on earth?

Juliet shut the dishwasher. ''I'll put on her pajamas later.'' She started fussing around the kitchen, wiping invisible marks off the refrigerator, adjusting towels that hung perfectly straight, rearranging items on the counter. In a minute she would start alphabetizing her spice rack.

Clearly Nick made her nervous.

The knowledge pleased him in a perverse sort of way. At least she wasn't indifferent to him.

He edged casually behind her. ''I meant what I said earlier.''

''Oh? What was that?'' She had her back to him, scrubbing away.

Nick eased his hands over her shoulders, sliding them beneath her hair. ''What I said about wanting to kiss you.''

Juliet's spine snapped straight as a broomstick.

He crooked a finger to gently draw back a wing of her hair. Then he brought his mouth close to her ear and whispered, ''I still want to.''

A tremor rippled through her slender, luscious body. What cruel demon was making him do this? Nick wondered. Torturing both of them.

Normally he was a master of self-discipline, at controlling his needs or at least submerging them when the situation demanded it. Yet, trying to submerge his desire for Juliet only made it grow stronger, more out of control. The smell of her hair was like a dangerous, potent drug that weakened his will and sapped his strength to resist.

Nick buried his face in her neck and filled his

senses with the erotic, intoxicating scent of her. Then, slowly, he wheeled her around.

She came reluctantly. Her tense muscles and the stiff set of her shoulders revealed the inner tug-of-war pulling her in two directions at once. Nick could tell by her ragged breathing that she was fast succumbing to their chemistry, too. Clearly she also shared his opinion that surrendering to it would be a major mistake.

But Nick had made plenty of mistakes in his life. What did one more matter?

Juliet stared fixedly at his chest, refusing to meet his gaze, arms crossed in front of her like a barricade. Nick coaxed up her chin with one knuckle. When she finally lifted her eyes and he saw what was in them, he nearly lost control right there.

She wanted him. She wasn't too happy about it, but that didn't change the longing, the need that haunted her eyes.

Nick was afraid to come on too strong, afraid he might scare her off. He closed the gap between their mouths inch by excruciating inch. Reassuring Juliet she still had time to change her mind, to call a halt to this kiss.

She didn't move a muscle. But she didn't move away, either. Her incredible eyes were locked on Nick's like homing beacons, drawing him closer, leading him to the destination he was seeking. Gradually they filled his vision, cloudless sky, bottomless sea.

He swept a hand down her back, cupped the sleek swell of her bottom, pulled her as close as he could with her stubborn arms wedged between them. He gave her one last chance to turn her head, to push him away, to let out a murmur of protest.

Juliet stood silent, motionless except for the rapid rise and fall of her breasts.

Nick touched his lips to hers.

That simmering chemistry caught fire. Flames leapt inside him, blazing a hot trail of hunger through every cell in his body. He had to fight for restraint, to keep from plundering her mouth like a man parched with thirst. Good grief, how could one simple kiss turn into spontaneous combustion?

Her mouth was warm and soft, the way Nick had known it would be. She tasted as sweet as he'd anticipated—no surprises there. What surprised him, what shocked him to the core, was the explosive force of his own reaction.

Especially considering this kiss was a bit on the chaste side, by Nick's standards. Instinct cautioned him that coming on too aggressively was bound to spook Juliet. She wasn't like other women, the ones Nick had pursued and been pursued by. Juliet was innocent by comparison, though a woman who'd been both wife and mother hardly fit that description. Naive, then. No, that didn't fit, either. Not after Nick had so thoroughly disillusioned her.

Vulnerable? No. She'd suffered the tragic death of her husband, raised a child alone for three years. You had to be tough to survive all that.

Why, then, did Nick feel this compulsion to protect her, to go slow, when every hormone-charged cell in his body was raging at him to do the opposite?

He blended his lips lightly with hers, once… twice…three times. Juliet's response was tentative, almost shy. As if this were her first kiss ever.

Nick couldn't believe how much she excited him. No woman had ever affected him like this before.

Maybe he'd been going after the wrong women.

Whoa, hold on a second! Didn't that imply that Juliet was the *right* woman?

But she wasn't right, she was all wrong for Nick! She was too idealistic, too openhearted, too virtuous. She had a completely rose-colored view of the world, whereas his own turf included its seamy underbelly.

Nick only got involved with women who knew the score. He wasn't even sure Juliet knew what the game was.

That dash of cold reality finally restored common sense and control. Nick pulled back from their kiss, loosened his hold on her, let gravity pry them apart.

Juliet still had her arms crossed in front of her. A lucky break, because if she'd cooperated a little more, lifted her arms around his neck and pressed her lush breasts into him, Nick wasn't sure what it would have taken to stop him.

Her lashes fluttered open. As she gradually focused on him, surprise and uncertainty coalesced in her eyes, along with what looked like disappointment.

Or maybe his ego was just imagining it.

Somehow his fingers had gotten all tangled up in her hair. As soon as he freed them, Juliet stepped back. Not too far, because she bumped against the counter. But her body language sent an unmistakable signal. She wasn't about to let him kiss her again if he happened to change his mind.

Nick might just do that, if he hung around here much longer. "I'd better go."

"Yes." Barely more than a whisper, but the message came through loud and clear. *We shouldn't have done that.*

Juliet's lips glistened with moisture. Her breathing had slowed, but not by much. Judging by the glazed look on her face, she was still as shaken by their kiss as Nick was.

All the more reason to get out of here. Now.

"Thanks for dinner. For letting me spend time with Emma." He backed into a chair as he retreated.

"You're welcome." Regret descended over her face. For the time she'd given him with Emma? Or for what had just occurred between them?

Both, probably. Who could blame her for having second thoughts, after the way Nick had turned her life upside down and forced her to hide the truth from her own family? He hadn't meant to hurt Juliet, to complicate her life.

Of course, he hadn't meant to kiss her, either.

He should have satisfied his curiosity by now. He'd become acquainted with his brother's wife and child, which was way more than he'd intended when he'd first decided to track down the mysterious woman in the picture. Mission accomplished. Time to move on.

He just hadn't foreseen that saying goodbye would be so hard.

Juliet made no move to follow him to the door. Nick paused at the end of the kitchen. "It's supposed to snow tomorrow," he said. "I promised Emma I'd help her build a snowman." A pretty daring promise, considering he didn't have a clue how to make one.

Juliet nodded, lips pressed together as if in resignation. "I'm off work at three tomorrow. By the time I pick her up at Mom's, we should be home by three-thirty."

Please, she thought. Let the forecast be wrong.

She didn't want to see Nick tomorrow, the next day or any other day for the remaining duration of her life. He stirred up desires that shocked her, turned her into an entirely different woman from the one she'd always been. He made her feel out of control. Shameless.

If only she hadn't gone to Nick's motel room that night to learn the truth. If only she hadn't slipped in the street so that he'd been forced to reveal himself by rescuing them.

If only he hadn't come looking for her in the first place.

"Why *did* you?" Juliet murmured, hugging herself tighter. She didn't realize she'd spoken aloud until Nick stopped, turned, stepped back into the kitchen.

Uncertainty creased his forehead. "Why did I *what?*"

She should have known he would have superhuman hearing.

She forced her arms to relax. "Why did you come looking for me after you found my picture?"

Nick hesitated, apparently conducting an internal debate over what to tell her, then he said, "I couldn't figure out why Brad had left that picture for me." He shook his head. "What did it mean? What was I supposed to do with it?" He shrugged. "For a while I didn't do anything. An assignment came up. I had to go overseas for a while."

The way he said it revealed that it hadn't been a pleasant experience. A bleak, far-off shadow drifted through his eyes.

They moved into the living room. "What happened overseas?"

Nick gave a dismissive swipe of his hand. "It doesn't matter now."

"I'd say it does."

He grimaced. "Not to anyone but me. And the families of the innocent people who got killed."

"Oh, Nick." Juliet covered her mouth.

Nick recognized the swift stab of shock, of revulsion in her eyes. And she wasn't even aware that it had all been his fault.

"We were sent to the Middle East. Four of us. I was the leader." He paced across her living room, blind to the cozy furnishings, the treasured knickknacks, the Christmas stockings Juliet had hung by the fireplace. "The American consul general had been kidnapped by a group of rebels trying to overthrow the government. In exchange for his freedom, they demanded the release of one of their leaders from prison. Their government doesn't negotiate with kidnappers. Neither does ours. We went in to rescue him."

It sounded so simple. It should have *been* simple. Except he had made the bad mistake of trusting the wrong person. It was a decision that still haunted him months later, still punished him with nightmares.

Juliet's face was ashen, her eyes wide with dread. "What happened?"

"They were holding the diplomat inside the house of a village leader who sympathized with the rebels. A man I assumed was one of his enemies sneaked us inside. But then he betrayed us. We'd no sooner untied the diplomat than we were attacked from inside the compound. It was a setup. An ambush." Nick brushed a hand over his eyes, but he could still see the whole disaster with horrifying clarity. "Two of my men were hit, along with the diplomat. But that wasn't the worst of it.''

Guilt settled even more heavily on his shoulders, a weight he would have to bear for the rest of his life. ''Somehow we made it out of the compound, into the village and headed for the river where a speedboat waited for us. The rebels followed, blasting away with their machine guns. They could see we were going to escape. Out of desperation, they unloosed everything they had on us. The village…caught fire. Bullets were flying everywhere. People died. All because I'd been stupid enough to lead my men straight into a trap.''

A tear slid down Juliet's cheek. She dropped a hand to Nick's arm. ''You can't blame yourself for what happened.'' Her chin quivered as she said it.

She couldn't understand. She hadn't been there. She wanted to let him off the hook because she was a kind person, but Nick's conscience was a much tougher judge.

''We got the diplomat out, and though my men were injured, they all made it out alive.'' Not much consolation, when he considered the death and destruction they'd left behind. ''When I got back to Washington, my boss insisted I take a three-month leave of absence.''

Nick left out the part where he'd stormed around Donovan's office, slammed his fist against the wall, demanded the okay to go back and settle the score with the bastard who'd betrayed them. Donovan had refused him—and ordered Nick to take time off.

''I still had the picture of you.'' He let Juliet think he'd stuck it away in a drawer somewhere, didn't tell her how he'd gotten in the habit of carrying it with him, how he hadn't been able to get it out of his mind.

Play TIC-TAC-TOE and get FREE GIFTS!

HOW TO PLAY:

1. Play the tic-tac-toe scratch-off game at the right for your FREE BOOKS and FREE GIFT!

2. Send back this card and you'll receive TWO brand-new Silhouette Intimate Moments® novels. These books have a cover price of $4.25 each in the U.S. and $4.75 each in Canada, but they are yours to keep absolutely free.

3. There's no catch. You're under no obligation to buy anything. We charge nothing — ZERO — for your first shipment. And you don't have to make any minimum number of purchases — not even one!

4. The fact is, thousands of readers enjoy receiving books by mail from the Silhouette Reader Service™ months before they're available in stores. They like the convenience of home delivery, and they love our discount prices!

5. We hope that after receiving your free books you'll want to remain a subscriber. But the choice is yours — to continue or cancel, any time at all! So why not take us up on our invitation, with no risk of any kind. You'll be glad you did!

YOURS FREE

A FABULOUS MYSTERY GIFT!

**We can't tell you what it is…
but we're sure you'll like it!**

A FREE GIFT —
just for playing
TIC-TAC-TOE!

The Silhouette Reader Service™ — Here's how it works:

Accepting your 2 free books and gift places you under no obligation to buy anything. You may keep the books and gift and return the shipping statement marked "cancel." If you do not cancel, about a month later we'll send you 6 additional novels and bill you just $3.57 each in the U.S., or $3.96 each in Canada, plus 25¢ delivery per book and applicable taxes if any.* That's the complete price and — compared to the cover price of $4.25 in the U.S. and $4.75 in Canada — it's quite a bargain! You may cancel at any time, but if you choose to continue, every month we'll send you 6 more books, which you may either purchase at the discount price or return to us and cancel your subscription.

*Terms and prices subject to change without notice. Sales tax applicable in N.Y. Canadian residents will be charged applicable provincial taxes and GST.

If offer card is missing write to: Silhouette Reader Service, 3010 Walden Ave., P.O. Box 1867, Buffalo, NY 14240-1867

BUSINESS REPLY MAIL
FIRST-CLASS MAIL   PERMIT NO. 717   BUFFALO, NY

POSTAGE WILL BE PAID BY ADDRESSEE

SILHOUETTE READER SERVICE
3010 WALDEN AVE
PO BOX 1867
BUFFALO NY 14240-9952

NO POSTAGE
NECESSARY
IF MAILED
IN THE
UNITED STATES

The more Nick had studied Juliet's image, the more drawn he'd felt toward it. The more compelled to solve its mystery.

"Since I was stuck with the time off, I decided I might as well try to find out who the woman in the picture was." Lo and behold, here she stood in the flesh, her hand curved around Nick's arm while she studied him with those captivating eyes that had peered out from the photo.

The picture hadn't done her justice. Juliet was even lovelier in person. And no film could capture her warmth, her goodness, her inner beauty.

No wonder Brad had looked so crazy about her in their wedding picture.

Nick could see the picture on the coffee table, just past Juliet. She turned around to see what had caught his attention.

"Oh." She let go of Nick, walked over and picked up the framed photo. Her lips pursed with unhappiness while she scanned it. "I can't even look at this now without feeling like a fool," she said. "Like Brad was playing a huge joke on me, and I was too blind to realize it."

"He wasn't faking what he felt for you." Nick moved beside her. "Anyone can see that."

Juliet set down the picture with a bang. "You're the one who told me Brad was a master at pretending to be what he wasn't."

Nick shook his head. "He wasn't pretending when it came to his feelings for you."

Juliet made a scornful sound. "How would *you* know? I wasn't even important enough for Brad to tell you about our marriage."

"You were important." Nick grasped her shoulders and swung her around to face him. "Trust me."

Juliet's lips parted in surprise. Nick was a little startled himself by the forceful ring to his declaration. A declaration that maybe revealed more than he'd intended.

Juliet seemed to have that effect on him. He was always blurting out more than he meant to when he was around her. He should leave right now, before he confessed any more of his deep, dark secrets.

Besides, it would give him practice saying goodbye.

Chapter 8

"Mommy, look! We built a snowman!" Pink-cheeked with excitement, Emma tugged her mother across the new-fallen snow in their yard.

"He's a wonderful snowman!" Juliet inspected their creation with an admiring eye. "Does he have a name?"

"Mmm...Nick!"

Standing off to one side, the other Nick swept into an elaborate bow. "I'm honored," he told Emma, looking pleased.

She giggled.

Juliet muffled a sigh. It wasn't easy to harden her heart against a man who could make her daughter laugh like that. "Here, Tinker Bell. I brought you a carrot to use for his nose."

While Emma traipsed over to put the finishing touch on "Nick," Juliet came and stood next to the real one. "Your namesake is certainly an original work of art," she said. "I don't believe I've ever seen a snowman with actual legs before."

"You haven't?" His dark brows climbed toward his knit watch cap. "Then what do they stand on?"

Juliet thought he was joking, then realized he was serious. "Are you telling me you've never seen a snowman before?"

His mouth quirked in a sheepish grin. "Guess I've spent way too much time in warm climates."

"What about *pictures* of snowmen?"

"Hmm…can't say I ever paid much attention to them."

"Not even Christmas decora—oh, that's right. You're not big on celebrating Christmas."

Nick opened his mouth as if to object, but all that came out was a white cloud of his breath. He shifted his sights across the front yard. Juliet turned, too, and together they watched Emma dance around in circles, her head tipped back, her tongue stuck way out to catch falling snowflakes.

This was the kind of heartwarming, home-movie moment that Juliet usually imagined sharing with Brad. Emma's first step, her first word…every milestone, every cute little thing she said or did always made Juliet wish Brad could have been here to see their daughter.

But now that vision had been spoiled by her discovery of Brad's betrayal. She'd believed he was the perfect husband. Once that illusion had been shattered, how could she go on believing he would have been the perfect father?

Juliet stole a look at Nick. He was watching Emma twirl around, a kind of rapt amazement chiseled on his features, as if he'd never seen such a clever, adorable child before. Despite the cold, a grateful warmth crept over Juliet.

Yes, she thought. You understand how special she is, too.

How could she not feel a bond with a man who appreciated how wonderful her child was?

Before she could stop them, a brand-new series of images barged into her mind. Only, this time, they were of Nick and her. Nick, sliding a comforting arm around her waist as they stood side by side on Emma's first day of school. Sneaking into Emma's room together, late at night, to slip money from the tooth fairy beneath her pillow. Tightly holding hands while they sat nervously in the audience at Emma's first ballet recital.

No! Juliet shoved the images aside as forcefully as she could. It was a dangerous game even to imagine Nick in their future. Dangerous for her peace of mind, for her poor battered heart. She'd already counted on the wrong man once. She wasn't going to do it again.

"Hi, Mrs. Ryan!" Zachary, the eight-year-old from next door, waved at her. He plowed a path over from his yard. His four-year-old sister, Amanda, floundered behind in snow that came up to her knees.

"Wow, Emma! I've never seen a snowman like *that* before!" Zachary's mouth fell open as he stared in awe.

"Me and Uncle Nick made it." Emma hugged herself with pride. "His name is Nick."

"Who, your uncle?"

"No, silly. The snowman!"

Juliet couldn't blame Zachary for looking confused.

"It's neat," Amanda announced with an emphatic bob of her head.

"Mommy, can I stay outside and play with Zachary and Amanda?"

"Looks like we've been dismissed," Juliet murmured to Nick. "Sure," she called. She started toward the house, assuming Nick was right behind her. "Want to rescue your scarf?" she asked over her shoulder. At the moment it was draped around the snowman's neck.

No reply. Juliet turned. Nick stood in the same spot as if frozen to it. Still watching Emma, though now with concern creasing his brow.

Juliet went back. "Nick? What is it?"

His eyes were serious when he aimed them at her. "Do you think it's safe to leave Emma out here by herself?"

Juliet darted a glance at her daughter. "She's not by herself. Zachary and Amanda—"

"Are only kids, too." Nick scanned the area as if enemy agents might be skulking behind nearby trees. "What if something happens?"

"Emma knows not to go in the street," Juliet reassured him. "They all do."

Nick didn't appear reassured. "I'm not talking about cars."

Click! Juliet made the connection. "You mean *kidnappers?*" An incredulous smile rose to her lips. Wisely she swallowed it. It was commendable of him to be concerned, after all.

"Um, we don't worry too much about kidnappers in Lake Andrew. This is a small town, remember, not the big city."

Nick wasn't impressed by her sociology lesson. His

jaw shifted stubbornly. "Kidnappers can operate any-where. Not to mention other unsavory types."

"You're right." Juliet nodded, touched by his pro-tectiveness. "But Emma knows not to take candy from strangers, or get into a car with them."

Nick narrowed his eyes. "She might not have any say in the matter."

"I appreciate your concern, but I'm not going to turn into a paranoid, overprotective mother. Not when the situation doesn't warrant it. Much as I'd prefer to keep my eye on Emma every single second, that wouldn't be good for her. She needs to learn inde-pendence."

"She's three years old, for Pete's sake!" Nick waved a corresponding number of fingers in front of her face.

"It's not as if I'm letting her hitchhike to the Twin Cities!" Juliet shot a glance in the children's direc-tion. Luckily they were too busy pelting each other with snowballs to notice the rising volume of the adults' discussion.

She pitched her voice deliberately low. "I let Emma play with the other kids in the front yard be-cause she's proved to me that I can trust her not to run into the street or wander off. And I check on her through the window."

"But—"

"Nick." Juliet swung up her gloved palms in a pleading gesture of exasperation. "Do you truly be-lieve I would do anything that would endanger my child?"

He opened his mouth, shut it, glanced at Emma, then back at Juliet again. "No," he said finally.

"She'll be fine," Juliet promised.

With one last, suspicious look around, Nick followed her as she started toward the house.

It tickled Juliet that he was so determined to look out for Emma. At the same time, he'd just given her proof of what completely different worlds they lived in. In Nick's world, he had to be constantly on guard, forever expecting the worst, never able to trust anyone.

Juliet didn't want any part of that world. She was still reeling from the terrible story Nick had told her last night, about the people killed during the diplomat's rescue. Such violence, such evil, such danger.

And her own husband had lied to her so he could go on being part of that world.

Better remember that, the next time she was tempted to indulge in ridiculous fantasies about tooth fairies and ballet recitals.

Nick figured he'd spent more time in kitchens during the last few days than he had the entire rest of his life. He'd always viewed them as strictly utilitarian—the room where food was cooked. Until recently, he hadn't realized they could be such pleasant places to hang out.

He sat at the pine breakfast nook in Juliet's kitchen, drinking coffee and keeping an eye on Emma through the window. He'd noticed that in Minnesota, people always seemed to have a pot of coffee on, no matter what time of day.

Juliet stood over by the counter, wrestling with something that looked like a big blob of dough. She'd tied her hair loosely back with a ribbon, and had changed into sweater and slacks instead of the skirt and blazer that Nick was starting to think of as her librarian outfit.

Funny. He'd never associated the word *librarian* with anything sexy before. From now on he would.

"What are you making?" he asked.

"*Julekake.*" Her slender shoulders moved up and down while she kneaded the dough.

"Yool-eh-kah-keh?" he repeated dubiously. "What's that?"

"Norwegian for Christmas cake. But it's really more of a sweet bread with dried fruit in it."

"You mean like fruitcake?" Nick asked warily.

"No." She smiled. "*Julekake* is a yeast bread. It's lighter in texture and flavor."

Whatever that meant.

"It's a holiday tradition," she went on. "My grandmother made it every year, then my mother and now I do. I'm going to take some over to her when it's finished. And some for Tim and Suzanne."

Tradition. Home-baked bread. Concepts as foreign to Nick as that funny Norwegian word. "Did Brad like *julekake?*"

He wasn't sure what had made him ask. There was just so much of his brother's life that was a mystery to Nick. And only one person who could fill in the missing pieces.

Juliet went still for a couple of seconds. Then she resumed kneading the bread with what seemed additional vigor. Pounding, pulling, punching...

"Brad and I only had one Christmas together," she said. "But as I recall, he liked *julekake* just fine." She flipped the dough over and brought it down on the wooden board with a loud slap. "Of course, for all I know, he was just *pretending* to like it."

Uh-oh. Maybe this was the wrong time to ask about
Brad. But Nick doubted there would ever be a right
time. Besides, this might be his last opportunity. He
was running out of excuses to hang around in Lake
Andrew.

"How did you and Brad meet, anyway?" He
braced himself to duck, in case Juliet hurled that
bread dough at him.

She hurled him a reluctant look, that was all. "We
met in New York. I was there for a librarians' con-
vention, and Brad was there—" She stopped, shook
her head in amazement. "You know, I don't have the
faintest idea why Brad was really there. Now that I
know his import-export business didn't even exist."
She shrugged and went back to dividing up the bread
dough. "Maybe he was in New York to infiltrate the
United Nations or something."

"Unlikely," Nick pointed out.

"Nothing would surprise me anymore." With prac-
ticed efficiency, she plopped dough into four separate
pans, covered them with a dish towel and set them
aside.

Nick was about to prod her some more, but then
she continued. "Brad and I met when we both went
for the same taxicab. It was rush hour and raining, so
cabs were in short supply."

She poured herself some coffee, then sat across
from Nick. She picked at a loose thread on the quilted
place mat. "I'd spent all afternoon at the New York
Public Library and was on my way back to my hotel.
Brad was...well, I have no idea where he was coming
from or headed to. But he insisted we share the cab,
even though he'd actually grabbed it first."

Nick understood his brother's generosity perfectly.

When a gorgeous, dripping blonde slides into the cab beside you, you don't tell her she'll have to wait for the next one.

"We had a nice conversation in the cab. Not flirty or anything, just friendly. I remember thinking that what people said about New Yorkers certainly wasn't true." She sipped some coffee. "I got out of the cab first."

Her eyes intercepted Nick's over the rim of her mug. Glorious, flawless sapphires. If he'd been Brad, he would have leapt out of that cab after her.

"I thought that was the last I'd ever see of him." Juliet's eyes glimmered an even deeper blue. "But the next afternoon, when I walked out of the conference session, there he was in the hotel lobby, holding a big bouquet of roses."

Roses? Nick thought in astonishment.

A ghost of pleasure danced about her lips. "I didn't even get it at first. I thought it was just coincidence that he'd shown up there, that the flowers were for someone else. But then he handed them to me."

Nick felt like a Peeping Tom, watching the poignant, private memories soften her face.

She dabbed at her eyelids and cleared her throat. "Anyway, that was how it started. He took me to dinner, we talked until the sun came up, I spent the next three days with Brad instead of attending the conference."

"Then you came back to Minnesota?"

"Oh, yes." She traced the rim of her mug with one finger, smiling mysteriously as if she could see the past shimmering in the dark depths of her coffee. "I was so sure that was the end of it, that it had just been a casual fling for Brad, even though it certainly hadn't been one for me. I cried the whole plane trip home.''

Nick would never in a million years have let her get on that plane.

"A week later, I opened the door of the apartment where I was living, and there stood Brad. Before I could even catch my breath, he asked me to marry him.'' Her smile fell apart. ''So I did.''

Nick had made a rule about not touching Juliet again. But it was his fault she looked so unhappy. He wove his fingers through hers and contemplated them. ''You don't wear a wedding ring.''

''No.'' He sensed she was making an effort to keep her hand perfectly still. Not to pull away, not to react to his touch. ''About a year ago I took off the ring and put it away in my jewelry box. It just felt...like it was time.''

Nick reached across and gently brushed a streak of white powder from her cheek. ''Flour,'' he said by way of explanation.

''Oh!'' She made hasty swipes with her free hand, as if fearful her entire face was covered with the stuff.

''Just that one spot,'' he assured her. ''Oops, there's another.'' He dusted her soft skin. There hadn't been any flour in that second spot.

Juliet's flustered gaze intersected his, caught, held. Completing some kind of circuit between them. Nick felt a high-voltage current surging from her body to his and back again. It electrified him, sharpened his perception to record levels so that his senses instantly absorbed every tiny detail about her.

The tempo of her breathing, the homey smell of coffee and spices and fresh bread that clung to her clothes, the enticing female fragrance that rose from her hair and skin, calling to something primitive and urgent inside Nick.

He was acutely aware of every single wisp of fine, pale hair that escaped the ribbon to frame her face like a golden halo. He registered the exact curve of her earlobe, the perfect bow of her upper lip, and noticed for the first time how her irises shaded to an even deeper blue along their outer edges.

Her lips parted. She began to breathe faster, like Nick.

Something major was happening here. Something that scared the stuffing out of him. Good God, how could mere eye contact feel like they were running their hands all over each other?

He realized he was still holding hers. He untangled his fingers, quick, then pretended he needed both hands to lift his coffee mug.

Juliet's features resettled as if she were coming out of a trance. She blinked, glanced at her hand as if surprised to find it there at the end of her arm. She pulled it safely back into her lap and turned to stare out the window. Her profile was a perfect cameo against the snowy backdrop outside.

"Well," she said after a minute, "I've told you my story. Let's hear yours."

Nick snorted. "Haven't you heard enough of them?"

"Not enough nice ones. Tell me about you and Brad growing up."

He would have to dig deep for those. Their childhood was pathetically lacking in heartwarming family tales.

Nick hated to dig deep.

"We moved around a lot," he told her. "Most archaeologists stay in the same area for years, working the same site. But for my parents, the grass was always greener somewhere else." He pulled an ironic face. "Or the excavations were always more interesting, I should say."

"What places did you live?" Juliet wore a keen, bright-eyed look of expectation that made Nick feel he was bound to disappoint her.

"Africa, Asia, South America...by the time I turned eighteen, I'd lived on five of the seven continents."

She hunched her shoulders. "Sounds exciting."

"Yeah. But it had drawbacks, too. We would just get settled in some new place, Brad and I would make a few friends with the local kids, then *adios!*" He jerked a thumb over his shoulder. "Time to pack up and move somewhere else."

"What about school?"

"Pretty hit-and-miss. My parents never bothered waiting till the school year was over to relocate, so Brad and I were always the new kids showing up in the middle of the session, after the other kids were already established in their little cliques." Nick shrugged. "It was tough making friends."

After a while, he'd realized it was actually better that way. Fewer connections to sever the next time they had to move on.

"Our parents taught us some at home," he said. "Otherwise we never would have stayed caught up academically."

"Your parents taught you?" Juliet perked up with interest. Nick knew exactly what she was imagining. Some cozy scene with little Nick and Brad bent over a table while Mom and Dad hovered behind them, helping the two boys with their lessons. The proud parental smiles when the boys got the answers right, the patient, encouraging corrections when they didn't.

Nick didn't have the heart to disillusion her again. He spared her a truer description of the scene. Mom and Dad would have been the ones huddled over the table, completely absorbed by the work spread out in front of them. Little Nick and Brad would have been banished to the other room until they completed the demanding assignments they'd been handed.

Right answers weren't applauded, they were simply expected. Wrong answers earned frowns of disapproval and continued banishment until the right ones were produced.

A harsh education, but Nick had to admit, it had delivered results. When the time came, he and Brad could have gotten into any college they wanted to.

"What happened to your parents?" Juliet bit her lip. "I know they died...."

"I was nineteen. Back in the States to go to college. I was just starting my second year." Nick dragged a hand over his face. "My parents were killed in Africa by an anti-government faction who wanted all Westerners driven out of the country."

"Oh, no!" The color fled from Juliet's face.

"Several other archaeologists were killed, too, along with a bunch of the local workers."

"Brad?" she whispered.

"He was away at boarding school in the capital when it happened. He came to live with me afterward. I rented an apartment off campus, and the next year Brad started college at the same school I went to."

Juliet pressed her fingers into her temples. "Nick. My God, how awful for both of you."

He peered at her curiously. "Brad never told you all this?"

She clamped her lips and shook her head. "He said they died in an accident. It was obvious he didn't want to talk about it, so I never pushed him." Juliet's voice took on an edge. "I assumed it was because their deaths were still so painful for him, but now I realize it was just one more clue to his past that he was determined to hide from me."

"Neither of us talked about it much," Nick said lamely.

Juliet sent him a sharp look. "It's nice of you to defend your brother, but there's not much excuse for him not even explaining it to his own wife." Sympathy mellowed her resentment. "How absolutely tragic. I can't even imagine what it would be like to lose my parents that way...."

Strange, but when his parents had died, what Nick had mourned the most was the loss of any chance to ever develop a close relationship with them.

"That's probably why I joined the CIA after graduation." This was the first time Nick had said those words out loud, or even to himself. Back then he hadn't analyzed his decision, just gone on what his gut had told him was the right direction. "My parents weren't perfect, but they didn't deserve to die that way. None of those people did. I wanted to do what I could to prevent that kind of senseless slaughter in the world."

A faint smile tilted Juliet's mouth. "Why, Nick Ryan, if I didn't know you better, I'd say you were an idealist."

"Me? Nah." He dismissed the label with a wave of his hand. "I don't believe we'll ever live in a perfect world, or that people will ever stop killing themselves for stupid reasons.''

''Then why do you do what you do?''

''Because...I'm well suited to it. I've lived all over the world, I'm used to adapting quickly to all kinds of conditions, and I picked up half a dozen foreign languages while I was growing up.''

Juliet shook her head. ''That makes you good at what you do. It doesn't explain why you do it.''

Dig deeper. She was always wanting him to dig deeper.

''Once in a while, I'm convinced I actually make a difference. That innocent people who might otherwise have died survived because of me.'' The bitter irony of that sucker punched him in the stomach. *What about the flip side of the coin, Ryan? That sometimes innocent people* die *because of you?*

He took a swallow of cold coffee. With forced nonchalance he said, ''Hey, someone's got to fight the bad guys, right?''

Juliet eyed him with that perceptive, X-ray intensity that made Nick want to dive under the table before she saw too much. ''But why does it have to be you?'' she asked.

Her question made Nick sit up straight with surprise. ''It's who I am.''

The answer seemed obvious, straightforward to him. To Juliet, it seemed to be disappointing. The intensity faded from her eyes, as if she were withdrawing to a private place inside herself.

Nick understood that need to withdraw. It was one of the rare things he and Juliet had in common.

She fiddled distractedly with the red-and-green ribbon tying back her hair. Now that he studied it more closely, Nick realized it was some kind of decorative holiday ribbon, probably meant for wrapping packages. He had to practically sit on his hands to stop them from reaching over there and untying it, spilling her luxurious blond hair over her shoulders where he could run his fingers through it.

What if Juliet actually let him? What if she let him kiss her again, take it one step further, then another…and another…?

Knock it off, Nick warned his libido. *You'd only hurt her if you followed through with it.* Juliet had been hurt enough already. By Brad. And by him.

Chapter 9

"Mommy, where does Uncle Nick live?"

Juliet paused while brushing Emma's hair. It was the afternoon before Christmas. In a few hours the whole family would gather at her parents' house for the Christmas Eve festivities.

Suzanne had phoned fifteen minutes ago. "These kids of mine are bouncing off the walls with excitement," she'd told Juliet. "What with Santa Claus coming and all that. Tim and I thought we'd take them sledding, to work off some of their excess energy before we go over to Mom and Pop's. Do you and Emma want to come?"

"I've got to finish making potato salad for tonight. But I'm sure Emma would love to tag along."

"Great! We'll pick her up in twenty minutes." Meaningful pause. "Is, uh, Nick coming tonight?"

Juliet had pursed her lips. "Gee, how could he refuse, after you and Mom both called separately to invite him?''

Suzanne had simply laughed and hung up the phone.

Her sister-in-law would be here any minute to pick up Emma. Juliet had been meaning to have a talk with her daughter about Nick. Her innocent question provided the perfect opening.

She resumed brushing. ''Uncle Nick lives in a place called Washington, D.C.''

''Oh! I've heard of that place.'' Emma nodded wisely.

''Yes, it's a famous city.''

''Is that where he goes to sleep at night?''

''You mean, when he leaves here? No, Tink. While he's visiting us in Lake Andrew, he stays in a motel.''

Emma tilted her head all the way back to peer up at her mother. ''Why doesn't he stay at our house?''

''Well...'' Juliet repositioned Emma's head so she could continue brushing. She had no intention of explaining to her daughter that the main reason Nick couldn't stay here was that Juliet wouldn't get a wink of sleep if he did. It was hard enough to control her attraction to him during the day. But during the long, dark hours of the night, with Nick sleeping just down the hall, Juliet's imagination would torment her with seductive visions.

He wouldn't sleep in pajamas—that seemed a sure bet. Maybe a skimpy pair of briefs. Most likely he slept in the nude, his massive shoulders sprawled across the bed, one of his size-twelve feet dangling over the side. Those pretty guest room sheets Juliet had bought on sale last spring would caress his naked skin, drape over him to outline every hard muscle and bulge of his long, lean physique.

With each tiny creak the house made, Juliet would tense, wondering if it was the sound of Nick entering her room. Coming to slide into bed beside her, to take her in his arms, to—

"Ouch! Mommy, that hurts!"

"Oops! Sorry, sweetie. I didn't mean to brush so hard." Juliet gave Emma's hair a few more guilty, much gentler strokes.

She realized Nick was attracted to her, too. She would have to be devoid of all her senses not to recognize that. The way he looked at her sometimes with those smoldering, secretive gray eyes made Juliet shiver. That one, fairly restrained kiss they'd shared the night of the tree decorating had nearly melted her into a puddle of slush at his feet.

That kiss had taken place four days ago. And every day since had required Juliet's all-consuming, iron-willed effort not to let it happen again.

Nick wanted her. As much as she wanted him. *That* was why she couldn't risk spending the night under the same roof with him.

Juliet set aside the hairbrush and crouched so she and Emma were eye to eye. The longer she postponed this talk, the more difficult it would be. "You know that Uncle Nick's going away soon, don't you?"

Emma's lower lip crept out. "But why?"

"Well…because he lives somewhere else."

"Why can't he live here?"

"Uncle Nick has a job in Washington, honey." A job that took him to all the violent, dangerous corners of the world. "Right now he's sort of on a vacation. But pretty soon he has to go back to work."

"But I don't want him to go away!" Tears filled Emma's eyes. "Uncle Nick plays with me, an' he fixed my merry-go-round and helped me build a snowman!" Her lip quivered. "Mommy, please tell him to stay. Please!"

As Emma's face crumpled, Juliet pulled her daughter into her arms. This was exactly what she'd been afraid of—that Emma would grow too attached to Nick. Juliet couldn't even comfort her with the promise that Nick would come back to visit them someday. She knew they couldn't count on him for that.

She stroked Emma's back helplessly. "He's not leaving right away, Tinker Bell. You'll see him tonight at Gramma and Grampa's, remember?"

With a sniffle, Emma nodded into the front of Juliet's blouse.

"And he'll be there at Christmas dinner tomorrow, too." She tipped back Emma's head and thumbed away her little girl's tears. "But he's not going to move here so we can see him all the time, okay?"

Not okay said Emma's mutinous expression. But at least she wasn't crying anymore.

"There's Aunt Suzanne, knocking at the door for you. Want to go answer it?"

Juliet lingered behind to collect herself. This cautionary chat with Emma had proved even more upsetting than she'd anticipated.

Worse, warning Emma that Nick would be leaving soon had made Juliet realize how much she herself was going to miss having him in their lives.

Her heart ached for her daughter. But it ached for herself, too.

The shortest day of the year was just past, so darkness had fallen by the time Nick arrived to pick up

Juliet and Emma at five o'clock. The darkness on Juliet's block, however, was lit up by the neon rainbow of blinking colors that blazed from the elaborate outdoor display across the street. Santa's entire workshop appeared to be set up on the neighbor's front lawn.

The first time Nick had come here, the neighbor's yard had reminded him of Vegas. Now the dazzling lights struck him as festive and not tacky at all.

He'd had a devil of a time persuading Juliet to ride with him to her parents' house tonight. Obviously she was trying hard not to depend on him for anything.

Nick should have been relieved by that. Instead he almost felt…hurt.

Another unfamiliar feeling dogged his steps as he strode up the front walk. It took him a moment to analyze it. For cryin' out loud! It felt like coming home.

Now, why would Juliet's little brick house, with light spilling out between its cutesy window shutters, stir that kind of reaction in him?

Nick had never let himself feel like this about places he'd lived as a kid, having learned that before long his parents would be dragging him and Brad somewhere else. And his apartment in Washington was simply a place to sleep, grab a bite to eat, recharge his batteries before taking off on his next assignment.

Maybe a sense of coming home didn't have anything to do with the actual structure you lived in. Maybe it was all about…people.

Nick wasn't sure he wanted to believe that. His long-standing policy of avoiding emotional attachments had served him well. Experience had taught him it was a mistake to get too close to anyone, because eventually either you left or they did. Sometimes they even died.

But Nick was also a hardheaded realist. Avoiding the truth, no matter how inconvenient it might be, never paid off. Inevitably it circled back to bite you in the hindquarters.

The truth was, he'd become way more attached to Juliet and Emma than he should have. With a bone-chilling jolt, he realized how much his niece had come to mean to him, despite his intention not to get emotionally involved. The idea of never seeing that adorable kid again was like the twist of a knife through his gut.

Well, okay. Emma *was* Nick's own flesh and blood. It made sense that he would be predisposed to develop a bond with her on some deep-rooted, genetic level. But it wasn't so easy to explain why Emma's *mother* should have become so important to him.

Could be the old forbidden-fruit syndrome. Not being able to have something inevitably increased its desirability, didn't it? Nick had known plenty of gorgeous women before. Maybe what made Juliet so special was the fact she was off-limits to him.

The last few nights, visions of her had drifted tantalizingly across his dreamworld, just out of reach. Long hair swirling around her beautiful face like spun gold…those haunting blue eyes, gazing deep into his as if she could see through to his soul…her soft, graceful hands reaching out to touch him…

A sudden stiff throb below his belt buckle warned Nick he'd better curb his runaway imagination before Juliet came to the door and found him in an embarrassing state of arousal.

Nick cursed. He didn't want to believe his feelings for Juliet ran any deeper than frustrated lust. He didn't want to feel connected to her on some complicated emotional plane that would only lead to trouble.

But he did.

The door opened. Juliet looked breathtakingly beautiful. Had she done something special with her makeup, something to give her that radiant glow as if she were lit from within?

Her hair shimmered loosely around her shoulders. Over glittery black slacks, she wore a midnight-blue sweater of some exotic, fuzzy material that looked soft as butter and clung to all the right places. Nick's fingers clenched against the urge to touch it. To touch her.

"Come in."

He noticed she and Emma had put up their own Christmas tree in the living room, a small one decorated with strings of popcorn and chains of red and green construction paper.

An odd piece of jewelry was pinned above Juliet's breast. Nick tried not to stare at it. "What is that? Poison ivy?" he asked, careful where he aimed his eyes.

"What?" Juliet glanced down in alarm. "Oh. No, it's a holly branch." She adjusted it with slightly offended pride. "My niece Karly made it in school and gave it to me last Christmas."

"It's very…unique."

"How tactful of you." If Nick didn't know better, he would swear Juliet was smirking. "Better start rehearsing a few exclamations of delight," she said. "I heard Karly was making something for you this year."

"For me?" Nick poked his chest. "You're kidding! She barely knows me. Why would she go and do something like that?"

"She wanted to make a gift for everyone in the family."

"But I'm not—"

"Yes," Juliet said with a jerk of her chin that dared him to argue, "you are."

Well, she was the expert on that subject, not him. Nick wasn't sure how he felt about his honorary membership in her family, though. Didn't that word imply obligation, commitment, settling down? Traps he'd made it a point to steer clear of in the past.

For some strange reason, the Hansens seemed determined to make him part of their clan. And the weirdest part was, Nick didn't even mind...much.

"Where's Emma?" he asked. He'd gotten kind of used to her running out to greet him whenever she heard his voice at the door.

"She went sledding with Tim and Suzanne's kids." Juliet headed for the kitchen. "They'll bring her to Mom and Pop's. Would you mind helping me carry some of this stuff to the car?"

Nick let out a whistle when he saw the array of dishes she intended to bring along. "What is all this stuff?" He lifted a cover and peeked inside. Some type of fancy fruit salad with whipped cream.

"Didn't anyone explain our Christmas Eve supper to you?" Juliet shoved a warm casserole dish into his hands. "It's potluck. We all bring a few different items and make sort of a smorgasbord."

"A few?" he muttered, arching one skeptical eyebrow.

"You know what a smorgasbord is, right?" She

juggled two dishes in her arms while she led the way out of the kitchen.

"Like buffet-style."

"Yes." She moved briskly down the front walk, waited until the dishes were arranged to her satisfaction on the back seat before she continued. "Smorgasbord is a Scandinavian tradition," she explained, rubbing her hands up and down her arms as they hurried back into the house. "And in our family, it started as a Christmas Eve tradition one year when Mom's oven quit working on Christmas Eve afternoon. She stuck the roast in, but no heat!"

Back into the kitchen for more dishes. "I was about fourteen that year," Juliet went on. "Pop and I jumped into the car and raced to the grocery store before they closed. We bought all kinds of cold cuts and cheeses and bread, and practically cleared out the deli section of various salads. All food that didn't have to be cooked, you see."

Nick marveled at the happy animation that lit her face as she remembered.

"Anyway, the meal turned out to be such a success, we decided to keep doing it every year. We still buy cold cuts and cheese, but now we make all the salads and side dishes ourselves." She made one last survey of the kitchen. "That's everything, I guess. Oh, wait, I was going to bring a dress for Emma to change into."

Nick waited in the entryway jingling his keys. He had to admit, he was a little apprehensive about tonight. Confronting an armed adversary was one thing. Being surrounded by a boisterous group of friendly Hansens was another.

What did they want from him, anyway? All this

warm acceptance and welcome-to-the-family stuff
had to come with a price. Nick just couldn't get a
handle on what it was they expected in return. And
until he could figure that out, he couldn't quite let
down his guard around them.

As he shifted his stance, something caught Nick's
eye. He peered upward for a closer look. Then he
grinned.

"Sorry for the delay." Juliet hurried into the entryway carrying a tote bag. "We can go now."

Nick pointed straight up. "Is, uh, that what I think
it is?"

She craned her neck to look. Dangling from the
light fixture overhead was a sprig of green foliage tied
with a red ribbon. "Mistletoe?" Her mouth fell open.
"How on earth did that…?" Her cheeks turned the
same color as the ribbon. "Suzanne. She must have
hung it there when she picked up Emma this afternoon." Juliet dodged Nick's glance and reached for
her coat.

"Wait a second, now." Nick laid a restraining
hand on her arm. "I'm no expert, but aren't you supposed to do something when you're standing under
mistletoe?"

"Oh, that." She blushed even deeper. "Just a silly
tradition."

"Tradition? Silly?" Nick took her other arm and
gently swung her around to face him. "Juliet Ryan, I
can hardly believe what I'm hearing." A mischievous
elf whispered in his ear, goaded him onward.

Now that Juliet could no longer avoid his eyes, she
injected a feisty spark into her own. "Okay. You want
a kiss? Fine. Let's have at it." She puckered her lips
and pointed at them. Daring him.

One thing he could never resist was a dare. "It would be awfully presumptuous of us to break tradition, don't you think?" He tugged her closer, settled her hips against his.

Juliet's eyes darkened. Her breathing sped up. "Well..." She gulped. "Tradition is very important...."

"I couldn't agree with you more." Nick brought his face near hers, nuzzled her nose once or twice. The scent of her hair nearly drove him crazy.

Her fingers curled gently, tentatively around his biceps. "Just one, though."

"One...what?" Nick eased his hands beneath her soft, lush curtain of hair. Drew her closer, so he could feel her breasts nudging into his chest, feel her heart beating against his.

"One...kiss." Juliet's breath warmed his mouth.

The way she said *kiss* nearly sent Nick over the edge. "Just one," he agreed, a split second before he joined his mouth to hers.

But in that first explosive surge of desire, when her arms finally came around his neck, Nick knew that kissing Juliet once would never, ever be enough.

Chapter 10

Passion swirled through Juliet's limbs and made them tremble. The room was swirling, too. At least, that's what it felt like. She couldn't see because her eyes were shut tight.

She had to anchor her arms around Nick's neck to keep from dizzily melting to the floor. It was reckless to turn a playful kiss under the mistletoe into full body contact, but what choice did she have when the hard fusion of his mouth had sent her reeling into space?

It's not too late to stop! You can still break off this kiss right now, push him away, laugh it off! You can both still pretend this doesn't mean anything more than a little holiday fun.

She should listen to the voice of reason yelling inside her head. She was making a big mistake, snuggling closer against him, responding with a soft moan when Nick deepened their kiss.

The problem was, Juliet didn't *want* to stop. She didn't want to get off this whirling, exciting ride. She wanted Nick to keep kissing her, and she wanted to kiss him back, and she wanted—oh, sweet heaven, she didn't dare think about where she really wanted this ride to end up, because that might bring the whole thrilling spin to a screeching stop.

One kiss. That's all she'd promised him. But from the first moment his lips had touched hers, Juliet had known it wouldn't stop there.

His tongue teased her lips, gently parted them. A ripple of need, sharp and vital, traveled straight to the core of her being. When he sought her tongue with his, Juliet welcomed it eagerly. He tasted like peppermint—either toothpaste or candy canes. But it was the flavor of passion in his kiss that fueled her hunger for him.

"Mmm." A low growl of pleasure vibrated in his throat. Juliet felt it with her fingertips as she moved her hands over his neck. She wanted to feel all of him, every hard, masculine square inch. She arched her back and strained against him, wanting Nick to feel her, too.

He complied. His big, strong hands spanned her waist, nearly lifted her off her feet as he slanted his mouth to kiss her even more thoroughly. He slipped his hands beneath her sweater, and the first touch of his callused flesh against her bare skin made her gasp with delight.

"You're so incredibly soft," he muttered between her lips. "Just like I knew you would be...."

Juliet felt a wild leap of satisfaction to know that Nick had fantasized about this, too. Wanted it. Craved it as much as she had.

His fingers traced the outline of each rib as if he were memorizing her, gradually working his way upward. Her heart slammed against her rib cage like a trapped bird. Nick nudged his abdomen more suggestively against hers, proving the strength and urgency of his arousal.

For one fleeting moment, Juliet almost panicked. But then Nick's hands found her breasts, and whatever rational impulse had briefly possessed her was swept away by a tidal wave of blind, aching need.

Through the lace of her bra, his thumbs teased the swollen tips of her nipples, rousing them to hardened peaks. A moan that sounded like anguish rose from her throat. How could anything possibly feel this good? His touch turned her insides to liquid, ignited her nerve endings, made her clutch his shoulders even more desperately.

She wove her fingers through the short hair above Nick's collar, reveling in the bristly feel and in the rhythmic, rapid pulse in his neck. Her roaming fingertips encountered a tiny patch of whiskers he'd missed while shaving.

This should feel wrong. Juliet's conscience should be screaming that she had no business kissing him like this, running her hands over him, grinding herself against him like some kind of wanton woman.

But it all felt so intensely, utterly right.

Nick's fingers located the clasp of her bra. In two seconds he flicked it open. Probably had had lots of practice. But somehow she didn't care. Instead of a jealous pang, she reacted with a quick thrill of possessiveness.

He's mine, Juliet thought. Not yesterday, not tomorrow, but for now, right at this very moment, he belongs totally to me.

She dug her fingers into his rock-hard shoulders.

Then he was coaxing her bra aside, cupping her breast, dissolving every cell in her body into a pool of longing. Juliet's head fell limply to one side, like a sunflower drooping on a broken stem. Nick buried his lips in her neck, sending charge after charge of desire rocketing through her body.

He molded her swollen, heated flesh into the palm of his hand, first one breast, then the other. His roughened skin created an impossibly erotic friction against hers. Oh, dear sweet heaven, she wanted him so much....

"Juliet, look at me." Nick's voice was ragged, but carried a forceful demand that managed to penetrate her drugged cloud of passion.

Her eyelids felt weighted when she dragged them open. Nick was breathing hard, his eyes stormy with turbulence and need. His hands had gone still on her breasts. Juliet tipped back her head to bring his face into focus. A chill seeped around the edges of the hot, raging fever that had gripped her.

She wanted to look anywhere but into Nick's eyes, fearful of what she might see there. She forced herself to hold a level gaze, even as the fire inside her cooled to ashes.

"Juliet, we shouldn't do this. *I* shouldn't do this. It's not fair."

She didn't need to ask what he meant. He meant he couldn't offer her anything more than sex. A quick coupling, a mutual satisfying of physical urges. No violins and flowers, no whispered words of love, no promises of forever.

Funny. She'd known all along Nick wouldn't offer her any of those things. Wouldn't...couldn't. What was the difference? A few moments ago, she'd been willing to settle for whatever he was willing to give. The reflection of that stark, shameless knowledge in his eyes was what humiliated her the most.

Nick withdrew his hands. Juliet reached awkwardly around to refasten her bra, then pulled down her sweater to cover her naked torso. More humiliation.

"I'm sorry." Nick dragged a hand through his hair.

Juliet busied herself straightening her clothes.

"I shouldn't have got carried away like that." He ducked his head to see her face, but that didn't mean she had to look at him.

"We both got carried away." Juliet shoved her hair into some semblance of order. As she collected her scattered wits, reality sank in. Dear God, it was Christmas Eve! Her parents and Emma and the rest of the family were waiting for them, and here she and Nick were, groping in the entryway like a couple of hormone-charged teenagers! What would everyone think when she walked in with her makeup all smeared, guilt lurking in her eyes, lips still bruised and puffy from Nick's kiss?

She reached overhead and yanked down the mistletoe with a savage twist.

"That wasn't the cause of this," Nick said quietly. He took her hand and gently uncurled her fingers to rescue the unfortunate foliage.

"It's what started it." Her voice was wavering all over the place.

"No." After a moment's examination, he tucked the mistletoe into his pocket. "What just happened here started the first time we came face-to-face." He tilted her chin so the choice came down to meeting his eyes or closing her own. "It's true, isn't it?"

Juliet longed to deny it. But she'd blinded herself to the truth once before, even when all the inconsistencies in her marriage had whispered that something was wrong. And look how much ignoring the truth had eventually cost her.

"Just because we're attracted to each other doesn't mean we have to act on it," she replied, skirting a direct answer.

"No." Nick's finger twitched against the sensitive underside of her jaw. "But just because we tell ourselves that going to bed together would be a big mistake, that doesn't mean it won't happen, either."

Juliet's belly clenched into a hard knot of desire. She yanked her chin away. She wouldn't let Nick keep touching her, wouldn't let him see so deep inside her. She didn't trust him to get that close.

Even more important, she couldn't trust herself.

"We won't be going to bed together," she informed him tartly, pleased by the bold confidence in her voice, by the way it concealed the chaotic turmoil inside her. "Believe me. It's not going to happen."

Maybe she didn't sound as confident as she thought. A combative gleam lit Nick's eyes as if he intended to dispute her. Then challenge turned to speculation, as if he were rethinking his strategy. Regrouping before his next foray.

Well, there wasn't going to *be* a next foray. Not if Juliet had anything to say about it.

"I'm not getting involved with you. With anyone. I've learned my lesson." She reached up to adjust his shirt collar. Nick watched her, only his eye muscles moving.

"My mother would make a pretty good spy her-self." Juliet stepped back. "She'd spot that rumpled collar as soon as we walked in the door and figure out right away what we'd been up to."

"In that case, maybe you'd better check a mirror," Nick said.

She whirled to consult the mirror near the coat-rack. Crimson flooded her cheeks. Dear God, she looked like she'd just crawled out of the back seat of some boy's car! Hair tousled, lips swollen from Nick's kisses... "Be right back," she mumbled, grab-bing her purse and heading for the privacy of the bathroom to repair the damage.

But she couldn't forget that reflected image of Nick, hovering behind her in the mirror, amusement flickering on his lips as he watched her with that spec-ulative, almost predatory gleam in his eye.

Like a lone wolf, licking his chops.

The biggest mistake Nick had made this evening was kissing Juliet beneath the mistletoe. His second biggest mistake was agreeing to dress up as Santa Claus.

Juliet's father and brother had cornered him in the kitchen after supper. "It's gotta be you," Tim had insisted in a low voice so the kids couldn't hear him in the other room. "When I went to rent the costume, they only had one size left. It's too big to fit Pop."

Carl Hansen confirmed this with a solemn nod of his head. His eyes twinkled behind his glasses. Okay, so this was a conspiracy.

"What about you?" Nick asked Tim. "You're about the same height I am."

"Maybe if I was wearing elevator shoes, yeah."

Juliet's brother guffawed. "Besides, it won't fit me, either." He patted his prosperous midsection. "Afraid I've added a little weight this year. Even put on a few pounds from that supper we just ate."

"Which was delicious, ladies." Carl spoke for the benefit of his wife, daughter and daughter-in-law, the three of whom had also wound up in charge of cleanup.

"Womenfolk!" Tim let out an appreciative caveman grunt. "What would we do without them?"

Loaded down with leftovers, Suzanne jabbed him with her elbow as she walked past on her way to the refrigerator.

"Oof!"

"I'll tell you what you can do," she informed him. "You can pitch in and help."

"But sweetness, your father and I have a very important job to do." Once her hands were empty, Tim grabbed his wife and waltzed her around the kitchen. "We've got to talk old Nick here into playing Santa."

"Oh, stop that. Let me go!" Suzanne blushed furiously, but she was smiling.

Tim planted a noisy, lip-smacking kiss on her cheek before he released her. The look she fired back mixed amusement and exasperation and a far more profound, permanent emotion that stirred a twinge of envy inside Nick.

For the first time in his life, he wondered what it would feel like to have a woman look at him like that. As if he were the only man on earth she could ever imagine being in love with.

He stole a peek at Juliet. She stood at the sink with her back to him, up to her elbows in dishwater, avoiding his glance the way she'd done all evening.

How would she react if Nick swept her off her feet and danced *her* around the kitchen?

Something else he was never going to find out.

Tim clapped him on the back. "Looks like you're elected, Santa."

"Oh, no." Nick waved his hands in protest. "No me. I don't know the first thing about Santa Claus

"Nothing to it! Just repeat after me.... Ho. Ho. Ho."

How come Nick suspected this was some sort of initiation? A test to determine whether or not he had the right stuff to become a permanent member of this family.

As if he sensed Nick weakening, Tim moved in for the kill. He folded his arms with an elaborate sigh and shook his head mournfully. "Just think how disappointed Emma will be if Santa doesn't show up this year."

A low blow. But effective.

"All right," Nick agreed through gritted teeth. "Tell me what I'm supposed to do."

Approval flared in Tim's eyes. "Juliet can fill you in while she's helping you change into the costume."

"What?" She pivoted around in shock.

"The costume's upstairs in Mom and Pop's bedroom. Hurry now. Shh! Don't let the kids notice what you're up to." Tim ignored his sister's protests and hustled the two of them out of the kitchen.

Which was how Nick found himself partially undressed in an upstairs bedroom with her.

"Pillows—that's what we need." Once Juliet had surrendered to the inevitable, she'd settled right down to business. But she still hadn't looked Nick in the eye.

"Pillows? What for?"

She'd instructed him to pull on the oversize red trousers over his own pants. Nick wasn't sure if that was how Santa normally dressed, or whether Juliet simply wanted to avoid a glimpse of him in his underwear. Apparently she was the only member of her family who was worried about it.

"Santa's belly, of course."

"Huh? Oh, the pillows." Nick frowned. "Seems to me your brother could have fit into this costume just fine."

Juliet grabbed a pillow off her parents' bed and started to stuff it down the front of Santa's trousers. Right away she thought better of it. "Here. You do it."

"Like this?"

She hesitated. "No, more like this."

As she adjusted the pillow, her face turned the same color as the costume. Nick had to fight back a grin. She was so cute when she was being all prim and proper. The good girl. The well-behaved librarian.

What entertained him even more was that he'd seen the other side of her. He knew that when she let her hair down, so to speak, she could be as wild and uninhibited as any woman he'd ever known. She certainly turned him on a lot more, with those sexy little moans, those deep, moist kisses, the way she—

Whoa. Santa had better keep his mind on his reindeer.

"One more pillow, I think."

This time, Nick handled it himself.

"Here, pull on these boots."

"How? I can't even bend over anymore."

"Sit down, then. Put on your jacket and stick out your feet."

Nick had to admit, he rather enjoyed having Juliet dress him. Of course, he would have enjoyed it even more if she were *un*dressing him. Not much chance of getting that gift for Christmas, judging by the standoffish, touch-me-not way she was acting.

Nick wondered if she was madder at him or herself for that earthshaking, erotic encounter they'd shared.

She stood up and eyed him critically. "Hmm, not bad. I have to admit, you make a pretty respectable-looking Santa."

"I doubt I'll fool anyone."

"Aren't you supposed to be a master of disguise or something?" She rummaged around in the cardboard box that had held the costume.

"I flunked that class in spy school."

"You're good enough to fool the little kids," Juliet assured him. "And the bigger ones know they'd better play along, because otherwise Santa Claus will leave a lump of coal in their stockings."

"A lump of what?"

"Never mind. Here. Put this on." She handed him a curly white wig and beard.

Nick regarded them with distaste. "Do I have to?"

For the first time all evening, Juliet looked Nick straight in the eye. "You really don't have a clue about Christmas, do you?" Her glance was exasperated, but at least it was a start. "Santa *has* to wear a beard. It's in his contract."

Nick gingerly tried it on. "This thing won't stay put."

"Here's the adhesive that came with it." She twisted her lips. "Hopefully you're not allergic to it."

"Thanks. I think."

"Oh, for heaven's sake, you're making a mess of it. Let me do it." She grabbed the brush from his hand and used it to dab sticky stuff all over his cheeks.

"Careful! I want to be able to get this thing off afterward."

The smirk on Juliet's face did nothing to inspire confidence. "Now the wig. And the hat."

Once she had the whole getup adjusted to her satisfaction, she stood back to inspect him. Nick felt like the rear end of a donkey.

"Perfect," she said. Her mouth twitched suspiciously.

Nick scratched his beard. "This thing itches," he grumbled.

"Here's the bag with presents. One for each child. You read the name off the tag and hand it to them. And don't forget, you're supposed to be jolly. Lots of ho-ho-ho's."

Nick took the burlap bag from her hand. "Correct me if I'm wrong, but isn't Santa supposed to come while you're asleep?"

"He comes to your own house while you're asleep. He comes to Gramma and Grampa's right after dinner."

"Aha. I see. I think."

"It's a family—"

"Tradition," he finished for her.

Surprise arched Juliet's brow. "You're catching on."

"Just don't expect me to crawl up the chimney afterward."

"You go out the same way you come in, by the

front door. Then sneak around to the garage and ditch the costume before you come back inside.''

''What if this beard won't come off?''

''Oops! Almost forgot. Here, put this in your pocket. It's the adhesive remover.''

Nick scowled. ''Why do I suspect you'd have deliberately forgotten to give it to me if I hadn't asked?''

Juliet shrugged, but didn't deny it. ''I'll go down and make sure the coast is clear so you can sneak out through the kitchen. Then come around and knock at the front door.'' She started from the room, but turned back at the threshold.

A change occurred in her eyes, a kind of relenting. Her mouth softened, reminding Nick how fantastic it felt to kiss her. Not that he needed reminding.

''You know,'' she said, scratching her head, ''you're being an awful good sport about this.''

Nick could have sworn he heard grudging admiration in her voice. An exhilarating warmth spilled through his bloodstream. By God, he would jump through hoops of fire, if that's what it took to please her!

He would have felt better, though, if he hadn't heard her snickering all the way down the stairs.

''An' then after Santa Claus gave me a present, he said, 'Well, I have to go now. My reindeer's double-parked.''' Seated on Nick's lap, Emma was filling her uncle in on everything he'd missed. She hooked a curious finger into her mouth and peered up at him. ''What's double-parked mean?''

Nick's performance as Santa had been a rousing success, despite a few rough spots. Emma and the two younger kids, Kristi and Kurt, had been spellbound with excitement from the moment Nick had stepped through the front door, booming out a very credible "Ho, ho, ho!"

Karly and Kyle had hammed it up beautifully, playing along even though they'd recognized Nick behind that bushy snowfall of whiskers.

Shortly after Santa's departure, Juliet had jumped up from the sofa to intercept Nick when he'd emerged from the kitchen. "You were great!" she'd whispered, snagging his arm to pull him into an about-face. "But you've still got a patch of adhesive near your ear!"

She'd helped him remove it out in the garage, both of them shivering, laughing over his performance, warning each other to be quiet so the kids didn't hear them. Juliet had stood close to him, bracing Nick's jaw with her hand to remove the last persistent bit of adhesive. The shadow of his real whiskers had rasped deliciously against her palm while his body heat had enveloped her, tempting her to settle into it.

All it would have taken was the slightest pressure of her hand, the smallest angle adjustment to bring his head down to hers...

Safe and warm in her parents' living room, Juliet shivered. Would she ever be safe around Nick? Or would she always have to fight the overwhelming temptation to give in to her feelings for him?

Watching him now, while he held Emma on his lap and traded good-natured banter with the rest of her family, Juliet feared what the answer was.

She would *not* fall in love with Nick. She simply refused to. Period.

The emotions he stirred inside her were simply a

trick of her subconscious, that was all. Every year, she imagined what it would be like if Brad were still alive to share the holidays with her and Emma and the rest of the family. Now, here was a living, breathing stand-in who even bore a strong physical resemblance to her late husband. Was it any wonder that she'd subconsciously transferred some of her love for Brad?

No, not love. After all, Juliet hadn't loved the *real* Brad, she'd loved a figment of her imagination. And she most certainly did *not* love Nick. Whatever misleading emotions she felt for him would evaporate when he disappeared from her life.

That conclusion should have reassured her. Why did it make her unhappy instead?

Suzanne elbowed her. She was seated on the couch next to Juliet. "Nick's really great with Emma, isn't he?" she leaned over to whisper.

"Too bad he's leaving town in a couple days," Juliet replied under her breath.

Suzanne glanced at her in surprise. "That soon?"

"He's got to get back to his job in Washington."

"Oh." She shrugged. "Well, he'll be back."

"I wouldn't count on it." But she said it so Suzanne couldn't hear.

Juliet *wouldn't* count on it. Now that she'd heard more about Nick and Brad's childhood—the lack of roots, the constant moving, the parents who were so wrapped up in their careers—she understood why both of them had learned never to get too attached to any one person or place. No wonder neither of them could ever settle down, when their lives growing up had been so completely unsettled.

Even though Brad had chosen to marry, he still

hadn't been able to overcome his restless nature. He hadn't been willing to commit himself wholeheartedly to another person, or even stay put long enough to let his marriage take root. Instead, he'd hedged his bets, created a double life for himself so that he would always have a backup plan. An escape hatch.

And his brother was no different.

All at once the familiar, cozy atmosphere of her parents' house felt suffocating to Juliet. She couldn't bear to sit here one more minute, pretending they were all one big happy family now that Nick had been welcomed into the fold.

Part of her longed to expose this farce, to stomp her feet and yell that Nick wasn't going to stay part of their lives, that he couldn't be trusted any more than the husband who'd lied and betrayed her.

But the other part of her was stronger. The part that wouldn't dream of hurting her family by exposing Brad's treachery, by revealing that all their welcoming overtures to Nick had been in vain.

Juliet stood abruptly. "Come on, Tinker Bell. Time to go home."

"But Mommy—"

"You have to go to sleep soon, or Santa won't come back with the rest of your presents." This blatant manipulation bothered Juliet a bit, but not as much as the idea of prolonging this heartwarming, completely pointless charade.

Nick wouldn't be here next year. He wouldn't even be here next week. And the sooner everyone got used to that fact, the better.

She held out her arms to Emma. "Let's put your coat on."

Emma grabbed Nick in a stranglehold. "I want Uncle Nick to put my coat on."

"Fine." When Juliet glimpsed the question mark in Nick's eyes, she averted her gaze.

Her mother touched her elbow. "Are you feeling all right, dear?"

Everyone else in the room was moving, too, as if Juliet had given the signal to end the evening.

"I'm fine. Just tired, that's all." She dredged up a yawn to prove it.

Her mother wasn't fooled, of course, but she was wise enough to let it go. For now. "What time are you coming over tomorrow?"

Juliet shrugged on her coat. "What time's dinner?"

Her mother buttoned her up as if Juliet were six years old again. "I thought we'd eat around two."

"I'll be here by noon, then."

"And…Nick?"

Juliet sighed, tented her fingers against her temples. "I'm not sure what his plans are."

"Oh, he already said yes when I invited him." Dora fiddled with Juliet's coat collar. "I just wondered if he would be giving you a ride again."

Great. At the rate things were going, her mother would be ordering wedding invitations soon.

As she searched through the pile for Emma's boots, Juliet tried to console herself with the knowledge that she only had one more gathering to get through, one more family event where she would have to paste a smile on her face and pretend nothing was going on between her and Nick.

Not that anything actually was, of course.

Surely Nick didn't plan to hang around after Christmas…

No. Not a chance. All this family togetherness was a novelty for him, that was why he seemed to be getting into it so much. His leave of absence ended January 2, hardly more than a week from now. Surely he would have to return to Washington before then, to clean his gun or recharge his walkie-talkie or something.

If Juliet could just get through tomorrow, she would be home free. No more battling her own desires, no more struggling to keep Nick at a physical and emotional arm's length, no more suffering her family's transparent attempts to shove them together.

Right. All she would have to cope with was the hollow ache in her heart when Nick went away.

Chapter 11

Nick was used to saying goodbye. He'd been saying it to people all his life. Over the years it had gotten easy for him.

Saying goodbye to Juliet and Emma was going to be one of the toughest things he'd ever done.

He'd said goodbye to her family a few minutes ago, and even that had been no picnic. Christmas dinner was over, the presents had been opened, the debris from both activities had been cleaned up. Accompanied by Juliet and Emma, he'd left her parents' house in a hailstorm of farewells and shouts of "Merry Christmas!" and invitations to come back real soon.

Now, as Nick drove them home, memories of the day flash-forwarded through his brain. Emma's face when she'd ripped off the wrapping paper and squealed with joy over the toy puppy Nick had given her. The kids, fighting over the wishbone from the Christmas turkey. Carl Hansen's beaming pride when he'd taken his place at the head of the table and surveyed the lively crowd of children and grandchildren gathered around him.

Nick sidled a glance at Juliet. She huddled silently in the passenger seat. It was dark outside, but passing lights illuminated her delicately sculpted profile, turned wisps of blond hair into a halo.

An ominous weight settled in the pit of Nick's stomach. The moment was fast approaching when he would see Juliet's face for what might very well be the last time. He could kid himself, tell himself he'd be returning to Lake Andrew someday to visit Emma or take Juliet's family up on one of their invitations.

But Nick knew himself too well. His career had always come first. He wouldn't have taken this leave of absence if he'd had any choice about it, and he couldn't picture himself taking vacation time to come back here.

Once he was caught up with the demands of his work again, memories would fade. He would forget how much he enjoyed holding Emma in his lap, forget how desirable Juliet was, how decent and honest, how caring and compassionate. He would forget about how once, just for a little while, he'd felt like he was part of a family.

That ominous feeling grew stronger, like the beat of war drums closing in. Nick eased up on the gas a little.

He suspected Juliet had only agreed to ride with him to her parents' house today because otherwise she would have been pestered with questions about why she hadn't. Except for the brief period in the car, she'd kept her distance from him all day. With so many people at Carl and Dora's house, it hadn't been hard for her to steer clear of him.

Obviously she was determined to avoid a repeat of last night's encounter beneath the mistletoe.

"Awfully quiet," Nick commented.

Juliet started, then glanced around at the back seat. "She's dozed off, poor thing. No wonder, with all the excitement."

"I meant you," Nick said.

"Oh."

Well, that sure hadn't sparked much of a conversation.

"It was nice of your family to give me that sweater." Nick had been touched and surprised when little Kristi had shyly approached him, carrying a package with his name on it.

"You made a big hit with everyone." Juliet didn't exactly sound too pleased.

"I'm glad I remembered to buy them something." Nick had spent hours stewing over appropriate Christmas gifts. In the end, he'd chosen gourmet coffee for the adults and a video game the kids could share.

He hadn't given Juliet her present yet.

It took several trips to unload the car when they got home, what with all the presents and wrapped-up leftovers from Christmas dinner. Nick carried Emma inside.

Maybe it's better this way, he thought, gazing down at her sleeping face after he'd laid her on the bed. *He could just slip away without having to say goodbye.*

Take the coward's way out.

Emma sighed, rolled onto her side, curled up into a ball. She was still hugging the stuffed dog Nick had given her. An empty abyss opened inside him. He hadn't meant to let her become important to him. Starting now, he would have to pay the price.

Juliet tiptoed in and stood beside him. "Still asleep?"

"Yeah." His voice came out kind of funny.

She slid him a curious look as she leaned over Emma to ease off her coat and boots. "It's only six o'clock. I doubt she's down for the night."

While Juliet arranged a blanket over Emma, Nick glanced around the frilly pink little girl's bedroom, imagining what it would be like to imagine his niece here when he was thousands of miles away.

Juliet dropped a kiss onto Emma's forehead, then moved to the door and switched off the light. A wedge of illumination from the hall fell partway across Emma's face. Nick stared hard at her, burning her angelic features into his memory.

Ignoring the wrenching ache in his chest, he turned and walked from the room.

Time to tell Juliet goodbye. But there was something Nick wanted to do first. When they reached the living room, he dug into his coat pocket. "Here."

"What's this?" She eyed the small narrow box with suspicion.

"Your present."

Her eyes widened. "Nick, you didn't have to buy me anything."

"I know. That's not what Christmas is all about. But I want you to have this, anyway."

She accepted the box reluctantly. She'd kicked off her shoes, so the only sound she made when she walked to the couch was the swish of nylon-clad thighs beneath her black slacks.

Nick slid off his coat and draped it over a chair. He sat next to her on the couch. Juliet untied the ribbon and opened the gift as if cracking Pandora's box ajar. She gasped. Inside was a necklace—a simple gold chain. Elegant and straightforward and beautiful. Classy. Like Juliet.

"Oh, Nick, I can't accept this." She held it up so the light glittered off it.

"Sure you can."

"It's way too expensive."

"Let me help you put it on." He lifted the long, luxurious spill of hair from her shoulders, fighting the urge to bury his lips in that delicious little spot just below her earlobe.

"Nick, really. This cost too much money."

He sifted his fingers through her hair. So soft… "I'm new at this gift-giving stuff," he said, "but it was my impression that the person receiving the gift isn't supposed to pay attention to the price."

"Well…technically."

"Let's be technical, then." He lowered his head. Almost, but not quite, a nuzzle. "Put it on."

Nick chose to believe the reason her fingers trembled while she worked the clasp had something to do with the fact he was hovering so close behind her. Breathing down her neck, so to speak.

Her hair swept over his hands, one last time, as she turned around.

"It looks terrific on you," Nick told her. "But then, you could make even cheap costume jewelry look good."

"Thank you." She blushed, toyed with the gold chain. Then her head shot up. "Oh! I nearly forgot your present.'' She jumped up, crossed the room and opened a cabinet. She came back and handed Nick a flat, festively wrapped package.

He took his time opening it, knowing that once this ritual was over, he would have no excuse not to leave.

His present was a framed photograph of Emma, taken moments after she'd jumped feetfirst into a big pile of raked-up autumn leaves. The camera had captured her midlaugh, a radiant grin stretching from ear to ear. Her cheeks were rosy from the fall air. A breeze lifted her curls, which had bits of leaf clinging to them. Her merry blue eyes were so joyful, so full of life....

A terrible ache snagged inside Nick's chest. ''Thank—'' He cleared his throat and tried again. ''Thank you. I'll treasure this.''

He gazed at the picture. To his surprise, Juliet folded her hand over his. The first time she'd voluntarily touched him in the last twenty-four hours. Nick welcomed the tender warmth of her skin, the caring and understanding she conveyed with her gesture, the sense of connection it gave him.

But she was making what he had to do even harder.

He met her eyes. ''I'm leaving town in the morning.'' He hadn't meant it to come out so blunt, so harsh. But would it have mattered how he'd said it?

Juliet's hand clenched in a brief spasm. Nick figured she would let go of him now. But she didn't.

''I...sort of expected you would.'' A thread of something he couldn't quite identify ran through her voice.

Nick put his other hand over hers and squeezed. ''I'm afraid if I stay any longer...''

He didn't finish his sentence. He didn't need to. He could see in her eyes that she was afraid of the same thing. Letting each other get too close. Risking the chance that passion would get out of hand, destroying the emotional barricades they'd both built for protection.

He had to leave town soon anyway. Better make it right away, while they both had defenses left.

Nick swallowed. "I don't know when or if—"

"Mommy?" Emma's sleepy voice turned their heads toward the doorway.

Juliet slipped her hand from Nick's. It took her a second to assemble a smile for her daughter. "You going to wake up, sweetie?"

Emma skipped over to the couch and wriggled herself and her toy puppy between the two adults. Juliet curved an arm around her.

"Is Santa Claus coming again tonight?" Emma asked.

Juliet laughed. "No, he only comes once a year. I'm afraid you've got three hundred sixty-four more days to wait."

Emma's mouth formed an O of astonishment. "That's a long time!"

Juliet smoothed her little girl's hair. "It'll go by fast."

Emma cast a shy glance at Nick. "Know what I'm gonna ask Santa for next year, Mommy?"

"What's that, Tinker Bell?"

She nudged Nick coyly with her foot. "I'm gonna ask Santa if Uncle Nick can come live with us and be my daddy."

Dead silence.

Probably a close call as to whether Nick or Juliet

were more stunned. Nick hauled a deep breath into his lungs, but Juliet collected herself first.

"Emma," she said, framing her daughter's round cheeks in her hands, "I'm afraid Santa can't make that happen."

"But Mommy, if you're good, Santa *has* to grant your wish!"

"Not that kind of wish, sweetheart." Juliet exchanged a despairing glance with Nick. "You see, Uncle Nick lives someplace else. He'll still be your uncle, but he can't be your daddy."

"Why not?" Emma's lower lip pushed into a pout.

Help me out here! Juliet fired him a glare of panic. *This is all your fault!*

Nick shifted uneasily. Might as well get this over with. Though he would much prefer to face a firing squad.

He took Emma's hand and patted it. He still couldn't get over how small and perfect it was. "See, the thing is, Emma, I have to leave tomorrow. I won't be seeing you for a while."

To his dismay, her lip began to tremble. "But Uncle Nick, you can't go away," she wailed. "I want you to stay and play with me some more."

Juliet looked as if she were trying to keep her own lip from quivering.

Nick made another attempt. "Honey, I have to go back to my job." He patted her hand faster. Like that would help. "People are counting on me."

Two perfect teardrops glistened in her woeful blue eyes. "But *I'm* counting on you, too."

"I know, but it's not the same. It's—" *Okay, Ryan, let's hear the end of that sentence. How is it different?*

"Uncle Nick, can't you just stay a little while more? Please?"

"Emma, I—I—"

One tear slid down her cheek. Then the other.

Ohhh, boy...

She clutched his sleeve. *"Pretty plee-e-eeze?"*

Nick would have sold out his country rather than deny the pleading in those irresistible, tear-filled eyes.

"Okay," he said. Anything to make her smile again.

Juliet shot a warning glance across the top of Emma's head. "Nick," she whispered, "don't make promises you won't—"

"I'll stay until New Year's Day." The words raced out of Nick's mouth before he could snatch them back.

"Hooray!" Emma bounced up and down. Her smile shone through her tears like sunlight on morning dew.

Every muscle in Nick's body unclenched a little. The ominous throbbing in his head subsided, replaced by a feeling like relief.

Big deal, so you dodged the bullet this time, his conscience sneered. *A week from today you're still going to find yourself boxed into the same corner, only, with no way to weasel out of it again.*

Nick's time was running out. This one-week extension only postponed the inevitable. And seven extra days around Juliet and Emma were just going to make it that much harder to leave them.

Thunderclouds gathered on Juliet's brow. Obviously she was having similar thoughts.

Late afternoon on New Year's Eve. The clock was ticking down in more ways than one, Juliet reflected.

The end of the year, the start of a new one, approaching. And tomorrow, Nick would walk out of their lives for good.

All week long she'd kept reminding Emma that Nick would be leaving soon. She'd hardly needed to remind herself. Standing behind the counter at the library, Juliet would emerge from a sort of trance to find herself staring at the clock on the opposite wall, watching its hands creep slowly around.

Bringing the moment of Nick's departure closer... closer...closer. Tick...tick...tick.

Part of her wanted to speed that clock up, to march over and whirl its hands at high velocity so the moment she was dreading would finally arrive. Once Nick was gone, she could finally start the business of forgetting him.

Hopeless. She would never forget him. Somehow Nick had managed to reach the part of her she'd sworn no man would ever reach again. He'd shattered her illusions, destroyed her faith in love and marriage, then made her care for him.

Damn him anyway.

Juliet's mother had phoned her at the library earlier this afternoon to say she was taking Emma with her on some errands, and would drop her at home afterward. So Juliet didn't need to come by and pick up Emma after work.

Juliet had the impression that Nick had spent a lot of time at her folks' house this week while Emma was there. She hadn't asked her mother about it for fear of inciting her matchmaker instincts to riot. But Emma was always full of Uncle Nick stories when she got home.

Juliet had only bumped into him a couple of times since Christmas. She assumed Nick was trying to make it easier on both of them by keeping his distance, and for that she was grateful. But she also missed him.

"Get used to it," she warned herself as she pulled into her driveway at dusk.

Her house was dark, empty, lonely. Juliet walked around switching on lights. Even though she was hardly in the mood to celebrate, she wished she'd been able to come up with plans for tonight—some distraction to take her mind off tomorrow's awful ordeal.

But her friends all had New Year's Eve plans of their own. Tim and Suzanne were driving down to a party in Minneapolis, leaving their kids overnight with Juliet's parents. Maybe she would take Emma over there after supper for a visit.

Except maybe her parents had invited Nick over. No, if that were the case, they would have invited Juliet, too. She had no idea what Nick's plans were for this evening. Other than packing his suitcase.

The bottom dropped out of Juliet's stomach. Dear God, how was she going to get through saying goodbye to him?

A knock at the door made her blink back her tears. Must be her mom with Emma. Juliet's mother would immediately demand to know what was wrong. Only, why didn't Mom just walk in, instead of knocking?

It was Nick on her doorstep. Juliet's stomach and several other vital organs immediately began to perform flip-flops.

"Hope I'm not too early," he said.

He was dressed up in a sport coat and light blue

shirt. The porch light cast the spectacular terrain of his features into even more rugged relief. His jaw was freshly shaven, and a bottle of wine nestled in one arm.

Desire made Juliet's mouth water. "Early?" she echoed blankly.

"For dinner," he clarified.

"Dinner?"

"You...did invite me for dinner tonight." His dark brows lifted into slight question marks.

"I did?" For heaven's sake, she was starting to sound like a parrot! She stepped aside to let him in.

He entered warily, as if checking for an ambush. "You left a message at my motel this afternoon. Inviting me here for dinner."

"No, I didn't." But she was starting to suspect who might have.

"You didn't?" Caution blended with surprise.

Juliet folded her arms. "I've got a pretty good idea who did, though."

A light came on in those guarded gray eyes. "Your—"

"Mother," they both said at the same time.

Juliet flung her arms in the air. "Terrific. Now she's gone too far. If she was going to set us up, the least she could have done was provide dinner."

Nick sniffed experimentally.

"No, I'm not cooking anything. Emma and I were going to eat leftovers tonight." Juliet paused. "Speaking of Emma..." She dashed for the phone, punched out her mother's number. "Mom?"

Just then, someone else knocked on her door. Grand Central Station around here. She nodded at Nick's inquiring gesture. He went to answer it.

"Mom..." Juliet shielded her mouth and whispered furiously into the receiver. "Did you call Nick's motel and leave a message inviting him to my place for dinner?"

"Why, no, dear."

Juliet heard the shuffle of feet in her entryway. She craned her neck to see who it was. Some guy in a uniform.

A uniform?

"Uh...you didn't call Nick and leave that message?"

"No, dear. Suzanne did."

"Suzanne?"

It was a chauffeur's uniform the man was wearing. Juliet glimpsed the cap clutched under his arm. He had a round, cheerful face and thinning brown hair combed forward in an out-of-date style. Both men were watching Juliet, Nick with a very odd expression on his face.

"Mom, where's Emma?"

"She's right here, of course. Helping me fix supper."

"Uh, Juliet..." Nick scratched his head.

"Supper?"

"Don't worry about a thing, dear." How could her mother manage to sound so innocent and smug at the same time? "Just relax and have fun."

"Fun?" Juliet nearly screeched. "Mom, what are you—" She yanked the phone from her ear and gaped at it in disbelief. "She hung up on me!"

"Good evening, and Happy New Year," the chauffeur said brightly, folding his hands in front of him. "My name is Terence and I'll be your driver this evening."

Juliet shook her head in confusion. "Driver?" Uh-oh.

"He's, uh, got a limousine parked outside."

"A *limousine?*"

Nick massaged the base of his neck. "Seems your family has arranged a little New Year's Eve surprise for us." His mouth quivered as if he were trying not to laugh.

"First, I'll whisk you away for a wonderful dinner at the Lakeshore House," Terence announced with enthusiasm. "Then it's off for a sleigh ride across the lake."

"Look," Juliet said, trying to rein this in before it got completely out of hand, "there's been some mistake."

"Oh, no, I don't think so." With a frown, Terence pulled a card from his pocket and consulted it. "You're Nick and Juliet Ryan?"

"Well, yes, but—"

Once again he was all smiles. "Then it's no mistake. This entire evening is a gift from—" he checked the card again "—the Hansen family!"

Nick shot Juliet a grin. "Gosh, isn't that swell of them?"

An intimate dinner at the most romantic restaurant in town? With a man she was trying desperately to push out of her mind, her heart, her fantasies?

Followed by a sleigh ride across a frozen lake, with the air so cold, they would have no choice but to snuggle close together to conserve body heat and keep from freezing....

"Swell," Juliet muttered. "Just peachy."

Nick was touched by the way Juliet's family had conspired to push them together this evening. Of course, he realized full well their attitude toward him would have been far different if they knew what he did for a living. No way would they encourage Juliet to get together with someone who was constantly away on secret missions, for whom death and danger were simply part of his job description. Part of who he was.

The Hansens were wasting their time anyway. Juliet had made it plain she had no intention of marrying him or anyone else, not after what Brad had done to her.

Not that Nick planned to propose, of course. Juliet deserved far more than he could offer her. Still, the idea of marriage didn't freak him out the way it would have once.

Wait a second. *Marriage?* The old ball and chain? Happily ever after and all that fairy-tale nonsense?

Get a grip, Ryan, he warned himself. You're allergic to marriage, remember?

Must be the champagne getting to him.

It was quarter of midnight. Nick and Juliet sat in the back of the limousine, sipping bubbly out of crystal glasses. The Hansens had clearly sprung for the most extravagant New Year's Eve package. A special dinner at the Lakeshore House, then a horse-drawn sleigh ride across the lake, with bells jingling and stars twinkling overhead and Juliet cuddled beside him under the thick wool blanket provided by the sleigh driver.

Nick had behaved like the perfect gentleman he wasn't. He hadn't tried to grope Juliet's sexy knee under the blanket or slide his hands anyplace else they didn't belong. He'd been sorely tempted, though.

Now the evening seemed to be drawing to a close, unless Terence had orders to drive them to New York City to watch the ball drop above Times Square at the stroke of midnight. No, the limousine was coasting to the curb in front of Juliet's house.

Terence hotfooted it around the car and whipped open the door for them. "Thank you so much," Juliet told him as he helped her out. "We had a wonderful time."

Nick thought that might be a slight exaggeration on her part. Through the course of the evening, Juliet had seemed anxious to ensure not one square inch of her lovely anatomy came into contact with Nick's.

But, as always, she was polite.

"Thanks." Nick palmed Terence a generous tip as he climbed out of the car.

Terence clicked his heels together and gave them a hokey bow. "Happy New Year to both of you."

"Same to you." Juliet held out her hand. Instead of shaking it, Terence kissed it.

Oh, brother, Nick thought.

They started up the front walk. "Good night!" Juliet waved as the limo glided off. "Well, that was certainly an experience, wasn't it? I've never—" She broke off with a frown.

"What is it?" Nick instinctively touched her elbow.

"Nothing, I…just thought I left the living room light on, that's all."

A faint, eerie glow came from inside the house, but not a hundred-watt-bulb kind of light. "I'll check it out." Nick moved ahead.

Juliet followed close behind. "It's probably burnt

out, that's all. I doubt it's some enemy agent lying in wait for us.''

A chill of dread slithered down Nick's spine. She could joke about it, but the fact was his job put not only himself but everyone he loved in danger, too.

This was the first time Nick had ever fully comprehended what that meant.

Maybe because he'd never lov—*cared* about anyone like this before. Except for his brother, who'd been trained to watch out for himself.

All the more reason for Nick to cut his ties with Juliet and Emma for good. He wouldn't be able to stand it if anything happened to either of them.

''Give me your key,'' he whispered.

''Oh, for heaven's sake.'' Juliet reached past him and unlocked the door. ''If it's a burglar, the last thing we want is to surprise him.''

''Look, stay here.'' He gripped her arms and held her in place, as if to make sure she stuck to this spot. ''Wait here until I check it out. Please,'' he remembered to add.

''All right, but hurry! It's cold out here.''

Nick went in.

A moment later he came back.

''Is it safe? What's that funny look on your face? Nick, what's wrong?'' She pushed past him. ''Do I hear music?''

Nick followed, a grin spreading toward his ears. Juliet halted stock-still at the entrance to the living room, staring. At the ice bucket of champagne on the coffee table. At the candles placed strategically around the room, waiting to be lit.

The glow they'd seen from outside came from a small camping lamp that gave off just enough romantic light so they wouldn't trip over the furniture. Mood music drifted out of Juliet's stereo, something syrupy with lots of violins.

"What on earth—?"

"There's a note." Nick indicated a piece of paper on the coffee table.

"I'm not sure I want to read it." But she picked it up anyway. "I'm going to kill them," she said through gritted teeth. She handed the note to Nick.

He scanned it. His grin got wider. "So your folks are going to keep Emma overnight, huh?"

"Subtle, isn't it?" Juliet flopped into the recliner chair without taking off her coat. "Better run while you can. They've probably arranged for a preacher to show up here tomorrow morning to perform the ceremony."

That farfetched possibility should have made Nick want to bolt out the door. But it didn't. "Be a shame to let all this go to waste, after all the trouble they went to."

"All the scheming, you mean." Elves had also left a heart-shaped box of chocolates next to the champagne. Juliet nabbed one and bit into it. "I can't believe my own family would gang up on me like this," she said, chewing.

"I think it was pretty nice of them." Nick settled himself on the couch.

Juliet swallowed. "I don't get it." She shook her head. "Doesn't it bother you that my family is trying to rope you into marriage?"

"They wouldn't be, if they knew who I really am. *What* I really am." He reached for the champagne bottle.

"You're right." Her agreement stung, even though

it was true. "But that doesn't excuse all this—this—" She waved her hand to encompass the candles, the champagne, the whole crazy evening. "This meddling."

Nick finessed the champagne cork. "Look, what's the big deal? We play along, drink some champagne, make them happy. Tomorrow I leave, and pretty soon they'll forget I ever existed."

Juliet recoiled as if he'd slapped her. "You're wrong," she said, her face pale as parchment. "They won't forget you."

"Well, okay." *Pop!* went the cork. "I'm sure they'll remember the time Brad's brother showed up for Christmas, but—"

"Do you think Emma's going to forget about you, too?" Juliet clutched the arms of her chair. "Do you think you can just blow right out of her life and she'll get over it? After all, she's only a kid, right? Give her a new toy to distract her, and she won't even notice you're gone."

Nick set down the champage bottle with a hard *thunk.* "That's not fair." Guilt prodded him between the shoulder blades, anyway.

"You're the one who's not being fair!" Anger restored the color to Juliet's cheeks. "You waltz into town, charm the socks off her so that she's crazy about you, then tell her, 'So long, kid, it's been fun.'"

Nick catapulted to his feet. "I didn't intend for this to happen. The last thing I want to do is hurt her. Or you."

"We're not talking about me."

"Aren't we?" Nick grabbed Juliet's wrists and hauled her to her feet. What the hell was wrong with him anyway? Manhandling her like this.

But it made him crazy that she thought he didn't care. That he wasn't torn up inside, too, knowing that twelve hours from now he would be on a plane carrying him out of their lives at six hundred miles an hour.

Juliet's eyes were electric with shock, with anger, with something that looked like anguish.

She thought he didn't care? Nick was about to show her otherwise.

As he brought his head swiftly down to hers, he glimpsed awareness on her face. Maybe even eagerness.

Then his lips were crushing hers, her arms were chained around his neck and their bodies were molded together so intimately, it would have taken surgery to separate them.

Somewhere, a clock began to chime midnight.

Chapter 12

The violins Juliet heard came from her stereo. The fireworks were out in the street, where the neighborhood had erupted in a flurry of whoops and bangs and whistles at the stroke of midnight.

The voice commanding her to stop kissing Nick right now, before it was too late, came from inside her own head. She knew she ought to listen to it, to uncoil her arms from around his neck and back away before this kiss got completely out of control.

Kiss? That was an understated description of what they were doing. It was more of a frenzied mingling of hands and mouths, a hot, molten collision of two bodies straining desperately to merge together.

Dear heaven, how she wanted him! She'd hoped by avoiding him for the last week, her longing for him would go away. Instead, it had only grown more powerful, more demanding. She was afraid of the feelings he stirred inside her, afraid of where they would lead. Afraid of where she knew they wouldn't.

Nick was leaving tomorrow. In all probability, Juliet would never set eyes on him again, never feel his hands in her hair or his warm breath on her mouth. She would never experience the exciting thrill of his caresses except in her imagination.

Knowing that broke her heart.

What did she have to lose, then, by surrendering to the passion that was gathering force and fire with each passing moment? Her heart was already broken. Didn't she deserve this one night of ecstasy? One glorious night of freedom to respond fully to Nick without considering the consequences, without fearing the risks...

She would never feel this way about another man. Didn't she deserve to make love with him just once?

Nick dragged her coat off her shoulders, pinning her arms to her sides. He deepened their kiss, exploring every secret corner of her mouth. Juliet twined her tongue hungrily around his. A soft moan escaped her throat. With her breasts pressed into his chest, she could feel the rapid hammering of his heart.

Nick cradled her face in his hands and finally broke their kiss. "This is crazy," he panted. "We have to stop this, unless..."

His unspoken question hovered between their lips. Juliet gazed into his eyes. She couldn't focus too clearly, not with his face two inches away. But in those smoldering, turbulent depths she saw her answer.

Nick had powerful feelings for her. Not powerful enough to keep him here, but there was a strong element of caring and tenderness in them. If his desire for her was purely physical, he wouldn't have made it this easy for her to call off this madness.

Easy? Ha! Halting this prelude to lovemaking would require every last shred of her self-control.

But Juliet didn't want to end it. The passion she and Nick shared was strong. The pleasure they could give each other tonight would be strong, too.

It would have to be. Because it would have to last her the rest of her life.

Juliet edged backward. Disappointment clouded Nick's features, but he released her at once. She struggled with her sleeves, got her coat the rest of the way off. Then tossed it aside, not even bothering to aim for the nearest chair.

She stepped into Nick's arms again.

Surprise flared in his eyes, followed quickly by pleasure. He held her close, hugged her till she could barely breathe. A long tremor shuddered through him.

"Are you sure?" he asked, pulling away to peer at her. A strand of black hair fell across his forehead. "Because if you're not, I don't want to—"

"Shh." She crossed his lips with her forefinger and smiled. "I'm sure." No doubts, no guilt, no regrets. She was going into this with her eyes wide open. This time she knew and accepted the terms of the commitment she was making. The commitment to let Nick go tomorrow, without trying to wheedle any empty promises out of him.

Desire leapt into his eyes. With one swift movement he swept her off the floor and carried her toward her bedroom. Juliet linked her arms around his neck, her heart beating like hummingbird wings. Her glance fastened on one of Nick's shirt buttons. She imagined her fingers, working that button open, proceeding to the next one, then the next....

A wave of dizziness engulfed her. Good thing Nick was carrying her.

The room was dark when he laid her gently on the bed. "I want to be able to see you, Juliet." The rumble in his voice gave her goose bumps. "Is it all right if I turn on this lamp?"

"Yes, I—I'd like to see you, too."

Nick fumbled with the bedside lamp switch. Juliet blinked at the sudden oasis of light. He towered above her, shirt rumpled, hair strewn every which way by her fingers. "We've got all those candles in the other room," he reminded her. "Should I go get them?"

"No," Juliet whispered, holding out her arms. "I want you to stay right here."

Nick's mouth curved with anticipation. "That's what I was hoping you'd say."

He lowered himself on top of her, bracing his weight on his forearms while he kissed her with leisurely deliberation. "You're so beautiful." He lifted his head and studied her before he kissed her again. "Inside and out. You're the most beautiful person I've ever known."

Tears rose to her eyes. "Oh, Nick, I—" Juliet swallowed, unable to finish.

"Hey, come on, now—what's this?" He lifted a tear from her eyelash, moving his big finger ever so carefully. He licked the tear, an amazingly erotic gesture that made Juliet's blood run hotter.

"Know what I think?" he asked.

"What?" Could that throaty seductress voice possibly belong to her?

"I think there are entirely too many clothes on

around here." With that, he levered himself off the bed. "I still have my sport coat on, for Pete's sake." He shucked it off. "Shoes. They have to come off."

Juliet kicked off her shoes, too, and used her toe to nudge them over the side of the bed.

Nick began to unbutton his shirt.

"Let me do that."

His eyes gleamed. "Your wish is my command." He lay beside Juliet, propping himself on one elbow so it was easier for her to reach his shirtfront.

She played out her fantasy, undoing his buttons one by one. Except her fingers hadn't trembled in her fantasy. She worked her way down to his belt buckle, hesitating only a second before she tugged his shirt loose from his trousers and finished the job.

Pushing the fabric aside, she pressed her lips to his bare chest. Nick gave a growl, low in his throat, but held himself still. Juliet shyly explored his hard, muscular contours with her hands, her mouth, her eyes. She skimmed her palms across the sprinkling of dark hair that tapered down to his belly, traced a faint ridge of scar tissue between two of his ribs.

She was afraid to ask how he'd gotten the scar, but she needed to remind herself why it could never work out between them. Even if a miracle occurred and Nick changed his mind about settling down.

Juliet had already lost one husband to the dangerous career he was so dedicated to. She would never, ever set herself and Emma up for another tragedy like that.

Face the truth. Don't ignore what Nick is, or pretend he's something he isn't. Don't make the same mistake you made once before.

She stroked his scar with her fingertips. "Where

did this come from?'' she asked, trying to sound casual.

"You wouldn't believe me." He lifted her hair, held it back like a curtain to see her face.

"Bullet wound? Knife fight?"

"I fell out of a tree when I was a kid. A branch stabbed me on the way down."

"You're right. I don't believe you."

"Believe this, then." In one smooth motion, Nick rolled on top of her. "I've seen and done a lot of rotten things in my life. Bad stuff has happened to me, and bad stuff has happened to other people *because* of me." The intensity in his eyes held Juliet perfectly still. "But you and Emma are the *best* things that ever happened to me."

He bowed his head, shook it, looked into her eyes again. "I never intended to mess up your lives, to hurt you, to tarnish my brother's memory. But I can't honestly say I'm sorry I ever came looking for you." His hands caressed her shoulders. "I'll never regret finding you, Juliet. Never." He squeezed her for emphasis. "Getting to know you and Emma has been the most precious gift I've ever received."

His image blurred through her tears. "Nick," she whispered. "Make love to me."

"Juliet." He trapped her name between their lips as he lowered his mouth to hers.

They took turns removing each other's clothing, one article at a time. Nick was used to holding himself in check, but this slow, provocative striptease tested him to the limit. He'd never actually seen much of Juliet's bare skin before, because of her bulky winter clothing. All those coats and sweaters, long skirts and warm slacks...

No wonder he could hardly wait to get her undressed.

Her mouth was warm and sweet, flavored with a hint of chocolate that made Nick greedy for more. Her gentle hands brushed across each newly exposed part of his body with an amazing instinct for what kind of touch would arouse him most.

He loved looking at her hair spread out across the pillow like blond silk, loved the little catch in her throat whenever he stroked one of her bare nipples with his fingers or tongue. And oh, how he loved the way her eyes got so big, how they glinted like rare sapphires, how they shone with eager need when he shed the last of his clothing and lay beside her naked, boldly erect.

When she slowly curled her fingers around him, Nick thought he was going to lose it right then and there.

"Whoa," he said through clamped jaws, carefully easing himself out of reach. "We'd better go slower, sweetheart, or this is going to be over before it's barely started."

"Can't take it, huh?" The satisfied glow in her eyes carried a trace of amused challenge.

Nick had never been able to resist a challenge. "We'll see who can take what," he growled. He plunged his tongue into her mouth, but it was hard to kiss her while she was giggling.

Her panties were the only barrier left between them. Nick flattened his hand on her stomach, felt the vibrations of her laughter. Then he slid his hand beneath the elastic band and located the secret, sensitive core of her passion.

Juliet stopped laughing.

Nick explored her gently with his fingers, teasing the hot, slick, velvety folds, savoring the way she writhed against his hand.

"Nick," she gasped, arching her back. "Please, I—I—"

"Say it."

"I want you...."

"You've got me," he said. "All night long."

He wouldn't let himself consider what would happen when the night was over. He didn't want to think about saying goodbye. He was too far gone to care about tomorrow, or the day after, or all the empty days that lay ahead without Juliet.

Right now the two of them were the only people on earth, and they both wanted the same thing. How could it be wrong to share it with each other?

Suddenly Nick couldn't tolerate even a flimsy barrier between them. He tugged on her panties. Juliet lifted her hips to assist him. He took his time sliding them down her long, sleek legs, pausing to leave a trail of kisses along her thigh...behind her knee...all the way down to her slender ankle. Just in case he had trouble finding his way back.

He didn't. He raised himself on one elbow to admire her, completely naked for the first time. Completely his. For tonight anyway.

Nick sucked a hiss of air between his teeth while he smoothed his hand over her flat belly, over every lush curve and tantalizing recess.

"I know I said this before, but it bears repeating." He shook his head in awe. "You are absolutely, incredibly, astoundingly beautiful."

Now he knew it wasn't only Juliet's face that turned pink when she blushed. She brought her hand to the side of his face. "You're pretty incredible yourself," she murmured. Stars shone in her eyes.

Nick turned his head to brand a kiss into her palm. He took hold of her hand and branded another on the inside of her wrist. He kept going, down the soft flesh of her arm, lingering at the tender crook of her elbow, proceeding all the way to her shoulder. Juliet made delicious little sounds in her throat.

He cupped the pale mound of her breast, enjoying her quick intake of breath when he stroked the hardened tip with his thumb. He brought his mouth to where his hand had been, kissing, sucking, flicking his tongue faster and faster across the straining peak while he kneaded her other breast with his free hand.

Damp heat rolled off her skin in waves. Her heart was pounding like artillery fire. Those little gasps came faster and faster. She curled her fingers through his hair, nudged her hips against him.

Nick felt his own desire building steam like a boiler about to explode. He tried to clamp down on it, to give himself more time to make it good for her.

But then she moaned, "Nick...now," and he knew time was about to run out.

He raised himself above her. When he saw Juliet staring up at him with those enormous eyes, so vulnerable and trusting for once, so stormy with passionate need, Nick felt himself drowning in their alluring blue depths. He sensed part of himself slipping away, never to be recaptured. The part he'd used to protect himself, to shield himself from more of the pain and loss and disappointment he'd known in his life.

Juliet lifted her arms around his neck and welcomed him into her body.

Nick groaned with sheer bliss. She was so hot and moist and tight. All her gentle swells and slender hollows somehow melded perfectly with his hard, bony angles. He moved slowly, giving her a chance to get used to him. From that first joining thrust they moved in sync together, eyes locked on one another, their breathing a ragged counterpoint.

"So...good," Nick panted. He tangled his fingers through her hair, fused his mouth with hers. Their tongues dueled, mimicking the rhythm of their bodies.

The pressure gauge inside him climbed higher and higher. He slipped a hand between them and caressed her breast. Juliet clutched his shoulders tighter. Faint whimpers emerged from her throat, till finally she had to tear her mouth from his and gasp for air.

"Nick, I—I—"

He heard something akin to panic in her voice. "Yes," he urged her. "Yes..."

The tempo of their movements accelerated. Now it was a race to see who got to the finish line first, a race Nick wanted to lose. But need was building inside him, desire clawing at him for release....

Then Juliet got a look in her eyes—an expression of wonder and disbelief, as if she'd just glimpsed the most magical, magnificent sight in the world. Her eyes closed as she flung her head from side to side on the pillow and cried out his name.

Nick rejoiced as wave after wave of pleasure spasmed across her face. Her throbbing contractions enveloped him, ignited a fuse deep inside him. And then all at once a ball of lightning rolled up his spine, urging him to thrust faster...deeper....

Lightning exploded in front of his eyes with a

blinding shower of sparks that sent him hurtling across the universe.

Bits and pieces of vision coalesced gradually. The tingling subsided and feeling crept back into various parts of his body. Now he felt parts of Juliet's body, too. His brain assembled all the sensory input from his nerve endings and informed Nick he was lying sprawled on top of Juliet and that he was probably squashing her.

He dragged himself off, rolled onto his back and curved an arm beneath her shoulders. "Wow." He blew a gust of air through his lips. "That was…truly amazing."

Juliet slung a limp arm across his chest. "Ditto."

Nick twisted his neck to peek at her. "That all you can say?"

She lifted her head from his shoulder. "I'm too exhausted to come up with anything more elaborate." She let her head drop.

Nick aimed a kiss at her forehead. "What a way to start the New Year, huh?"

"Beats champagne and noisemakers."

There was something tremendously sexy about the blond streamers of hair draped across his chest. Nick curled one around his finger. He couldn't believe how good she felt lying nestled here in the crook of his arm. Usually he couldn't wait to roll over and start snoring once the grand finale was over. But this time he wanted to savor every little intimate detail about his lover. He wanted to beat his chest and let out a Tarzan yell.

He wanted to make love to Juliet all over again.

How could he waste time sleeping, when they only had a few hours left together?

The thought was like a knife slash through his gut. From the moment he'd first laid eyes on her, Nick had warned himself against getting involved with Juliet. But somewhere along the way, he'd violated his own sensible policy of never letting a woman get close enough to get under his skin.

Juliet had not only got under his skin, she'd reached all the way in to his soul. She'd made Nick question himself, made him care about things that had never mattered before.

He hadn't been looking for a woman like her. He'd found her anyway, though. And the horrible irony was, now that he'd found her, he was forced to let her go.

The clock on the nightstand moved up one minute. Three forty-five a.m. Juliet had watched it change each of the last thirty-seven minutes. Each change bringing her sixty seconds closer to the moment Nick would tell her goodbye.

He curved around her, spoon fashion, one arm draped over her waist, his knees snuggled against the back of hers. He breathed steadily in her ear, plainly asleep. It was the first steady breathing out of either one of them since before midnight. Since before they'd made love the first time.

There'd been a second time, too. Even a third. Each time better than the one before, surprising them both. Each time had made Juliet feel closer to Nick, more connected to him in ways that went far beyond physical.

Unfortunately, she didn't want to feel close to him. She didn't want to feel connected. She didn't want to love him.

But she did.

The truth had crashed around her with breath-stealing force in the aftermath of that first incredible round of lovemaking. Once every cell in her body was no longer screaming for Nick's touch, once her senses were no longer swamped by the urgency of passion, Juliet had been able to hear what her heart was softly singing.

She loved Nick. She'd been fighting it since soon after she'd met him. But in the end she'd lost the battle.

Once again, that hopeless feeling descended on her, gripped her heart in a vise and squeezed. She and Nick could never have a future together. Part of the reason was him, because it wasn't in his nature to settle down or let himself become too emotionally invested in anyone.

Part of it was his career. Juliet would never risk losing another husband to the same dangerous line of work that had claimed her first one.

And part of it was her, because she'd been so badly betrayed. Nick had shattered not only Juliet's illusions about Brad, but also her faith in her ability to judge people. How did she know her heart wasn't making another foolish mistake by loving the wrong man?

Love wasn't the same thing as trust. And for her own sake as well as her child's, Juliet could never trust Nick to stay. Even if he should ever offer her that unlikely promise.

Juliet closed her eyes, knowing that the pain she felt now was a mere down payment of the price she would pay later.

Her eyes flew open right away. She couldn't sleep, not with dread whirling through her like a tornado, threatening to rip the precious memories of their love-making into tattered fragments.

Detail by detail, she took inventory of how it felt to lie in Nick's arms. The moist warmth of his breath stirring her hair...the exciting, masculine smell of soap and sweat mingling with the heat of his body...the delightful, secure pressure of his arm around her.

Prickling behind her eyelids signaled more tears. Juliet batted her lashes furiously to hold them back. She didn't want to wake up Nick with her sniffling, have to explain how this was both the most wonderful and most terrible night of her life, because of their lovemaking...because she wished she could lie here in the heavenly shelter of his arms forever...because in the morning he would leave...because she would never, ever love anyone again the way she loved him....

She must have dozed off. All at once light was filtering through the curtains. The bed felt cold. When Juliet rolled over, Nick was gone.

A lump of panic and despair leapt to her throat. So soon? She wasn't prepared yet, hadn't had a chance to steel herself for—

Then she saw the note on his pillow. The paper shook while she read it. "Juliet—Gone back to motel to change. Will stop here to see you and Emma before I go. N. P.S. Last night was..." Then he'd drawn a little picture of a haystack. No, wait, maybe it was supposed to be fireworks.

Juliet collapsed against the mattress, dismayed by how empty her bed felt without him. She couldn't believe Nick had managed to crawl out of bed, get dressed and write a note without waking her up. Mothers were trained to be light sleepers.

But he'd done it somehow, sneaked off like a thief in the night. Like a spy.

Nick took one more look at the picture of Emma that Juliet had given him for Christmas. This was all he would have of his little niece after today. He placed it in his suitcase, slipping it carefully between two of his shirts. Then he opened his wallet and studied the snapshot of Juliet that had led him here in the first place. Be nice if he had a more recent photo of her. But maybe it was just as well he didn't.

He put Juliet's picture back in his wallet, then shut his suitcase.

Today was his last day of exile. Tomorrow he would return to his job. The day after, he might be on his way to the Mideast, to Africa, southeast Asia…the possibilities were endless.

He waited for the prospect to whet his appetite for adventure. Nick wasn't used to being stuck in one place so long, spinning his wheels while others did the work he should have been doing. Why wasn't he looking forward to tackling his next assignment?

Maybe once he got past the awful farewell scene looming in front of him, he could muster some enthusiasm for moving on with his life.

Yeah. Right.

He took one last look around the motel room he'd called home for the past several weeks. Pretty spartan. Nick wasn't nostalgic about pulling up stakes and leaving a place for good, but he suspected this motel room might not be so easy to forget. He recalled the first time Juliet had come here, how she'd fainted into his arms when she'd mistaken him for her dead husband.

Maybe Nick should have denied everything, pretended he'd never heard of Brad, skipped town right away and left Juliet in peace. Didn't seem like much good had come of dragging everything out into the open.

But then he never would have held his one remaining flesh-and-blood relative on his lap. He never would have known what it felt like to be part of a family, even for a short while.

And he never would have experienced the incredible, satisfying thrill of making love with Juliet. A woman as eager to give as she was to take. A woman who wanted Nick for who he was, even after she'd made him dig down deep to expose the vast, bleak places he'd always kept buried inside.

Was he better off for having known Juliet and Emma? Right now it sure didn't feel that way to Nick. And all he'd done for them was complicate their lives, disillusion Juliet and, in the end, let them both down.

He dumped the suitcase in the trunk of his rental car, turned in his room key and drove to Juliet's house. He purposely hadn't allowed himself much time to say goodbye before he had to leave for the Minneapolis airport. Short and sweet, that's what he was aiming for. Though he knew the best he could hope for was short.

The pine needles of the wreath on Juliet's door were turning brown at the tips. A depressing appearance that matched Nick's mood. Across the street, the neighbor was dismantling his extravagant Christmas display. He waved at Nick when he saw him waiting at Juliet's door.

Nick waved back. Now, when it was too late, he was coming to appreciate small-town friendliness.

Juliet opened the door. For a few seconds they just stood there, studying each other, uncertain what to say. Juliet pushed back her hair. Her face was pale, making her somber eyes seem even larger. There were faint smudges beneath them, as if she hadn't gotten much sleep last night.

Nick knew for a fact she hadn't. When he remembered how they'd spent the hours after midnight, he was hit by an instant surge of desire that was almost painful.

"Come in," she said finally. "Emma's...in her room, playing."

Nick took a deep breath, but couldn't haul enough air into his lungs. "I don't have much time."

"I know."

They lingered in the entryway, keeping their voices low, as if they both realized it was better to get this goodbye out of the way first, before letting Emma know he was here.

Nick grasped Juliet's hands in his. They were ice cold, even though he was the one who'd just come in from outdoors. "I want you to know...how much last night meant to me."

She let out a long, unsteady breath. "It meant a lot to me, too."

"Making love was...different with you. Much more, somehow, than it's ever been before."

She pinched her lips together and nodded.

"I'm not good with words. And there are some I don't have the right to say." Nick raised her hands to his mouth, pressed a fierce kiss to her knuckles. "But I promise that I will never, ever forget last night, Juliet. I'll never forget you. Or Emma. Or the rest of your family.''

Tears rimmed her eyes. "We'll never forget you, either." Her voice climbed to a strangled squeak.

"Oh, God, Juliet." Nick bundled her into his arms. "If only there were some way…"

She shook her head against his chest. "We both know there isn't." His sweater muffled her words.

He clutched her tighter, as if that could still the trembling in her limbs. He felt like the world's biggest heel.

After a minute, Juliet pushed away. "I promised myself I wouldn't cry." She dabbed at her eyelids. "So much for promises, huh?"

Nick stuffed his hands in his pockets to keep from reaching for her again. "I'm sorry."

"For what?"

"For coming here and turning your life upside down. Ruining your memories of Brad."

"Don't be." Juliet flipped her hair over her shoulder, lifted her chin. "It's always better to know the truth. Even when it hurts."

Nick fisted his hands. "I never wanted to hurt you."

"I know that." Her face was calm now. Pale, but resigned.

Nick checked his watch. Not much time left. But there were a couple of things he still had to say. "You helped me…understand a lot about Brad," he told her. "And about myself."

Juliet almost smiled. "You helped me understand a lot, too."

Nick ached to touch her. But didn't dare. "I finally figured out stuff I've never understood. Like why

Brad didn't tell me he was married." Nick frowned. "I thought it proved we weren't as close as I always thought we were. That maybe I hadn't been a good enough brother to him."

Even now, Juliet couldn't let that pass. "You were a wonderful brother, Nick. Why else would Brad have chosen to follow in your footsteps?"

"I hope you're right." Nick rubbed his jaw. "And until I met you I also couldn't figure out why he set it up so I could find you, if he never returned from that last mission."

"Maybe Brad wanted you to know you hadn't been left all alone in the world." A sad smile touched Juliet's lips. "He knew I was pregnant. I'd like to believe he wanted you to discover you still had family somewhere."

"Could be." Nick had never looked at it that way before. "I think Brad was also hoping…that I would look out for you. Take care of you. Make sure you were all right."

The lines of strain around her eyes softened. "It would be nice to believe that. To know that Brad cared about me, despite the way he deceived me."

Impulsively Nick grasped her shoulders. "Brad loved you." The heartfelt conviction in his voice startled them both. "*That* I know for sure." How could any man in his right mind not be crazy about a woman like Juliet? "Maybe that's why he couldn't even risk telling his own brother about you."

Confusion pleated her brow. "What do you mean?"

"The unpleasant fact is, you make lots of enemies in my line of work." Just the idea of anyone trying to harm Juliet or Emma made Nick want to punch his fist through a wall. "Sometimes those enemies seek revenge. An agent's family can be vulnerable targets."

Juliet frowned. "You think Brad was afraid someone might try to harm me in order to get back at him?"

"Yes." Until he'd become involved with Juliet himself, Nick couldn't have comprehended the potential agony of losing her. "That's why Brad kept you a secret from the entire world, including me. To protect you." A drastic measure that Nick could understand now. "Brad wasn't willing to take even the remotest risk that word might leak out he had a wife. A wife someone might try to harm if they couldn't get to Brad himself."

Juliet's eyes held a glimmer of uncertainty. "I wish I could believe that."

"Believe it." Nick tightened his grip. "Brad wasn't one of the bad guys, Juliet. He made some bad choices, maybe, but he loved you. I'm absolutely sure of that."

If he left her with nothing else, at least Nick could restore some of her faith in the man she'd married.

Juliet sighed. Slowly she lifted her hands to Nick's chest. Her eyes searched his face helplessly. Hopelessly.

She didn't say a word. She didn't have to. They'd all been said. All except goodbye.

Nick jerked her closer. Somehow he forced it out. "I have to go."

"I know," she mouthed soundlessly.

A roar filled Nick's head like the onrush of a locomotive. Unable to stop himself, he seized Juliet in his arms, kissed her hair, her temples, her mouth in a desperate frenzy of need and longing. Juliet locked her hands behind his neck and held on as if she would never let go.

A gaping chasm of pain and emptiness opened inside Nick. He drew back his head, framed Juliet's beautiful face in his hands, thumbed tears from her cheeks.

The words tore from his throat, uncensored by pride or reason. "Come with me," he said.

Chapter 13

Go with Nick to Washington?

The stunned circuits in her brain whirred furiously, trying to sort out the implications of such a decision. What exactly was Nick offering her? Marriage? Some kind of temporary substitute?

It didn't matter. Either way, her answer would have to be the same. Juliet had made exactly one impulsive decision in her entire life—marrying Brad. Just look how that had turned out.

She unchained her arms from around Nick. Let her hands fall to her sides. Stepped out of his embrace.

"I can't." They were the two hardest words she'd ever spoken.

A whipcord of intense emotion lashed through his eyes. Disappointment? Maybe. Certainly not surprise. Nick knew as well as she did all the reasons why any future together was out of the question. Hopping on that plane with him would only delay the inevitable,

make their ultimate parting even more heart-
wrenching than it was now. Though Juliet couldn't
imagine feeling more miserable.

"Emma," she called, quickly, before Nick tried to
persuade her to come with him. She wasn't sure how
strong her own resolve was. If he touched her again
right now, whispered the right words into her ear, she
might just melt into a puddle at his feet.

They heard Emma skipping through the house.
Nick hastily rearranged his features.

"What, Mommy?" She braked to a halt at the entryway. "Hi, Uncle Nick!" Her cheeks dimpled at the
sight of him.

"Hello, Emma." Nick hesitated, then tousled her
curls. He let his hand linger on top of her head a
moment, obviously pondering that this might be the
last time he touched his niece's baby-fine hair or saw
her adorable smile.

He dropped to his haunches so he and Emma were
eye to eye. The stoic mask he put on didn't fool Juliet
a bit. He sandwiched Emma's small hand between
his. "I have to go back to Washington today, sun-
shine."

Any sun in Emma's demeanor immediately vanished behind a cloud. "But Uncle Nick, you promised
not to go!"

"I promised I'd stay until New Year's Day, and
that's today."

Emma threw her mother a pleading look.
"Mommy, tell Uncle Nick we want him to stay."

You have to get through this, Juliet ordered herself.
For Emma's sake. Do it.

She knelt beside her daughter. "Tinker Bell," she

said gently, "I told you Uncle Nick would be leaving soon. He has to go back to his job, remember?"

Emma's chin quivered. She glanced at Nick again, her eyes filled with tears and accusation. A finger inched into her mouth. "Wh-when are you c-coming back to v-visit?"

A muscle flickered along Nick's jaw, betraying his inner turmoil. "I don't know, Emma." He squeezed her hand. "Not for a long time, probably."

Emma's face crumpled. She launched herself at Nick, nearly knocking him over as he caught her. He regained his balance, hugged her close, patted her back while she cried. A flash of pure anguish contorted his chiseled features.

It was all Juliet could do not to collapse into a sobbing heap herself. "Emma." She pried her daughter away from Nick, knowing he would never have the heart to do it himself. "Say goodbye, sweetie. Uncle Nick's going to miss his plane."

"G'bye, Uncle Nick," Emma wailed, turning her face into Juliet.

"Goodbye, Emma." As if he couldn't resist, Nick fingered her golden curls one last time. He pushed himself to his feet and mumbled something Juliet couldn't quite make out. It sounded almost like "I love you."

She exchanged one final stricken glance with him over the top of her weeping child's head. Then he turned, opened the front door and walked through it.

At last Juliet could let her own tears flow freely. They trickled into Emma's hair. Above the sound of her daughter's sobs, she thought she heard Nick's car start up outside. After that…nothing. He was gone.

Juliet swung her little girl into her arms, carried her

over to the couch and cuddled her on her lap, rocking back and forth…back and forth…

It's over…it's over…it's over…

But Juliet knew the heartache was just beginning.

Emma finally lifted her head and sniffed. "Mommy, why do they call it goodbye?" she whimpered, rubbing her eyes with the back of her wrist. "'Cause it doesn't feel good at all."

Donovan rose, signaling the end of the debriefing. Papers rustled, chairs scraped backward, final gulps of coffee were swallowed. Donovan intercepted Nick on his way out of the conference room.

"Good job, Ryan." His boss stuck out his hand.

Nick shook it. He'd just returned yesterday from a ten-day undercover operation to ferret out the source of an intelligence leak from inside the U.S. Embassy in one of the former Soviet republics. Things had turned nasty near the end, but at least Nick hadn't had to shoot anybody.

The operation had been a big success.

"You ought to be proud of yourself," Donovan told him. "By the way, I intend to put a special commendation in your file."

Nick nodded in curt acknowledgment. "Thanks."

"Obviously that leave of absence did you a world of good." His boss winked. "Just like I told you, huh?"

"Yeah."

Donovan's pleased expression turned puzzled as Nick quickly made his escape from the meeting room.

Back in his office, he propped his feet on his desk, knocking over the stack of documents that had piled up in his In basket while he'd been away. He didn't bother to pick them up. The sickly, pale green walls closed in, made him feel claustrophobic. Why didn't this stupid cubbyhole of an office have a window anyway? Something Nick could sit and stare out of while he tried to figure out what the hell was wrong with him.

His mission had gone better than expected. Donovan had lavished him with praise. Normally Nick took great pride and satisfaction in a job well done, but this time his triumph felt hollow. Pointless.

Dropping his feet to the floor, he pulled out a drawer. Drew out a picture and set it on his desk. Leaned back in his chair to study it.

One corner of his mouth kicked up in unconscious reaction to Emma's irrepressible grin. It had been two weeks now since Nick had seen that sunny smile in person. Except the last time he'd seen her face, it had been covered with tears.

Guilt shifted uneasily inside him, like a hibernating bear that never quite fell asleep. Two weeks. Was that long enough for a three-year-old to forget him?

He wondered if she still played with that stuffed puppy he'd given her for Christmas.

Unable to stop himself, Nick tugged his wallet out of his pocket and removed the snapshot of Juliet. Even from a photo, those blue eyes still held the power to mesmerize him. His mind conjured up the memory of those same gorgeous eyes starry with laughter…smoky with passion…bleak with sorrow.

That hibernating bear inside him stirred wider awake.

Nick had known it wouldn't be easy to put Juliet and Emma out of his mind after he came back to Washington. He'd let himself get way too attached to them for that. But he'd believed, because he'd wanted to believe, that time would gradually fade the pain of leaving them.

Instead, he missed them more with each passing day.

Even during the time he'd been wrapped up overseas, focused on his assignment, they'd been with him somehow, almost like living presences. Almost as if they'd become part of him.

At night their images floated across his ceiling. The distant echo of their voices haunted his dreams. Sometimes he dreamed he was building a snowman with Emma, and woke up smiling. Other times he jerked awake sweating, his body hard and ready, tortured by erotic visions of Juliet that quickly disintegrated but left Nick wanting her with an ache that verged on excruciating.

He scooped up both pictures and stuck them back in his desk drawer. Out of sight, but never out of his mind. Or his heart.

Nick prowled his office like a tiger trapped in a cage. What would they be doing right now? He consulted his watch. It was an hour earlier in Minnesota, so that would make it about five forty-five. Allowing for the time it took Juliet to go by her mother's house after work to pick up Emma, they should be getting home right about now.

Nick had been staring at the phone a full thirty seconds before his brain even registered what he was looking at. Piece of cake. Just pick it up and punch in a string of numbers. Simple, right?

Not so simple. But he would go nuts if he couldn't talk to Juliet, make sure she and Emma were all right.

He grabbed the receiver and made the call before

he could change his mind. Listened to the phone ring once…twice…three times…

Juliet's answering machine picked up. Just the sound of her recorded voice was enough to drive a fist of need straight into Nick's gut. Panic quickly followed. What message should he leave? How could he possibly explain his reason for calling, when he didn't understand it himself?

When the machine beeped, he hung up. Where could they be? He checked his watch again. Ought to be home by now. Well, maybe Juliet had been delayed at her parents' house. He would try again in a few minutes.

Two hours and seventeen tries later, Nick's frustration and worry had reached the wall-climbing stage. Logic assured him there were a thousand rational reasons why Juliet wasn't home, or why she might choose not to answer her phone right now.

But logic didn't count when one of those reasons might be that some harm had befallen them.

He whipped out his wallet again, dug through it till he found the piece of paper he was looking for. He snatched the phone. On his eighteenth try, he punched out a different number.

The air was raw. Not as cold as Minnesota, but there was something about the leaden, overcast skies and the somber rows of gray granite markers that made the afternoon feel especially bleak.

The wind sneaked inside the folds of Juliet's coat like prying fingers, dried the tears on her cheeks to ice. Except for the hair whipping about her head and the trembling bouquet of daffodils cradled in one arm, she stood frozen as a stone monument, gazing down at her husband's grave.

Just his name and the dates of his birth and death. No sentimental inscription, nothing about Beloved Husband and Father. Of course, at the time Brad died Emma hadn't been born yet, and Nick hadn't known about his brother's wife. Still, there was something unbearably sad about seeing a man's life reduced to a pair of dates.

Juliet wiped tears from her eyes. For so long she'd assumed that Brad rested at the bottom of a foreign sea. She thought she'd been denied even the small comfort of a grave to visit. An exact spot on earth where she could go to feel his physical presence.

But then Nick had barged into her life and forced her to reexamine all her beliefs and assumptions about the man she'd married. Before he'd left Minnesota, Nick had told Juliet the name of the Washington cemetery where he'd buried his brother.

Nick. Juliet's spell of shivering had nothing to do with the cold this time. After Nick had left her and Emma, the first week of the New Year had passed in a blur of pain and sorrow. But as life had settled back into its comforting, familiar daily rhythms, gradually Juliet had been able to think about something besides the fact that Nick was gone.

She'd thought about Brad. About their life together, which had turned out to be so completely different from what she'd believed. She'd thought about the life they might have had together if Brad hadn't died.

His shocking deception would have had to come out eventually. What was he planning to do, maintain his charade of a double life until he reached retirement age? Juliet wondered whether she would have been able to forgive Brad for his lies if he'd finally confessed.

If he'd lived.

But at least she could forgive him after he died. That was the discovery Juliet had made about herself after time had had a chance to blunt some of the sharp misery she'd felt over losing Nick.

She needed to forgive Brad. Otherwise she would never be able to close the chapter of her life with him. And that meant she would never be able to close the chapter with Nick, either, since the two were so inextricably entwined.

Juliet knew she would never stop loving Nick. She would never forget him, never stop wishing that destiny hadn't placed them on paths that led in such opposite directions. Her one salvation was the desperate hope that someday she would find the strength to leave Nick in the past where he belonged.

She couldn't put him behind her, though, as long as the business that had first brought them together remained unfinished.

Closure. Isn't that what they called it? Not that Juliet believed life was doled out in neat packages you could wrap up and tie with a bow. In her experience, life came with lots of messy loose ends that stayed that way forever.

But Juliet's heart had compelled her to make this journey to Brad's grave. Call it the final act of her marriage. Delayed for several years by unavoidable circumstances, but something she still needed to do. For Brad. For herself.

She knelt beside his marker, grazed her fingers over the rough stone as the lettering blurred with tears. No sound came out at first, when she said her husband's name.

She told him about Emma. About how Nick had found them. About how hurt she'd been when Nick had revealed the other, secret half of Brad's life.

"I couldn't believe you'd lied to me. Betrayed me." The wind stole the words from her mouth, whipped them off into the cosmos. "But now I realize that people can't change who they are. Your career meant too much to you to give up. And I guess I did, too."

She inhaled a quavering breath. "Emma will grow up knowing you were a hero, Brad. As soon as she's old enough, I'll explain how you gave your life for your country. She'll be proud of you."

With a gentle, sad smile, Juliet traced his name with her fingertips. "I am, too," she whispered.

She laid the bundle of daffodils on his grave. The yellow blooms were a bright splash of color against the wintry, brown-tipped grass beneath them. The wind stirred their petals, creating motion, an affirmation of life in a place where everything lay so still.

Juliet straightened, cinched the belt of her coat, hugged her arms around her middle. "Goodbye, Brad." Once more, tears misted her vision. "I'll be back someday. With Emma." She pressed icy fingertips to her mouth, let a kiss fall to the flowers. "I promise."

She stumbled as she turned to go. Why hadn't she remembered to bring a handkerchief, a tissue, *something* to mop up the moisture leaking from her eyes? She ducked her head against the wind, aiming herself in the general direction of the parked rental car.

The next time she glanced up to correct her course,

she spotted a man standing beneath a nearby tree. Stark, bare branches jutted up against the pewter sky. He had his hands stuffed in his pockets, his collar drawn up around his neck. The hem of his black trench coat flapped in the wind.

The very picture of a spy.

Considering the setting, Juliet could have been forgiven for thinking she saw a ghost. This time, though, she knew who he was right away.

She halted in her tracks. Her breath froze in her lungs.

Nick.

Juliet blinked rapidly as he came toward her. His stride held a certain hesitation, as if he were having second thoughts about approaching her. A pressure that was both exquisite and agonizing piled up behind Juliet's breastbone till she thought she might fly apart at the seams.

Dear God, how she loved him!

"Juliet." Nick chose a position where several yards still separated them. He kept his hands in his pockets. "It's...good to see you."

Those piercing gray eyes thrilled her, terrified her. They'd haunted her dreams for weeks. With a sinking heart, she realized they always would.

Say something.

She gestured behind her. "I was visiting Brad's grave." *Brilliant, Juliet. What else would you be doing here?*

Nick nodded. "I saw you. I didn't want to...intrude, so I waited."

"How—?" She scooped a ribbon of blowing hair out of her eyes. "How did you know I was here?"

"I tried calling you last night. When I kept getting your machine, I phoned your parents."

"I see." *He called!* Juliet's heart soared.

Common sense shot it down. *Stop it, Juliet. Just because he called doesn't change anything.*

"I…gather you told your parents about me. About Brad." Nick raked a hand through his dark, wind-swept hair. "About everything."

"Not everything." Some matters were too private, too painful to discuss even with her family. "But they deserved some explanation for why you won't be back. Considering they had the impression that you and I… Well, never mind." Juliet fought back a blush. She lifted her chin. "I decided there have already been too many phony cover stories in this family. So I told them what I'd learned about Brad. And that you have the same job."

Nick's jaw shifted. "I'll bet they were thrilled to hear that." Beneath the sarcastic veneer was the unmistakable ring of regret.

"They were surprised, naturally." But had immediately rallied around Juliet with their love and support. Tears stung her eyes again.

"I'm kind of surprised myself." Nick hunched a shoulder. "That your mother would even tell me where to find you."

No doubt Nick's phone call had raised her mother's hopes for a reconciliation. But then, her mother didn't understand how dedicated Nick was to his career, or how fiercely he guarded his independence.

"Did you speak with Emma on the phone?" Juliet had left her with her parents.

"No." A shadow drifted over his rugged features.

"Your mother mentioned she was there, but I…thought it was probably best not to."

Juliet nodded. Emma was starting to bounce back after losing the newfound uncle she'd become so attached to. Juliet was grateful to Nick for not stirring up hopes in Emma that he was going to play an ongoing role in their lives.

"How is Emma?" he asked, swallowing.

"She's fine." Physically, anyway. And her tender, bruised feelings would heal in time, too. "She sleeps every night with that toy puppy you gave her for Christmas." A smile lifted one edge of her mouth. "She named him Nick."

Juliet had thought he would be pleased. Instead, he grimaced as if it pained him. "I miss her." It sounded like a confession extracted by torture.

Her smile slid off her face. "Emma misses you, too." *So do I.*

She'd given Nick his cue, the perfect opening to tell her that he'd also missed *her.*

He didn't take it. "When do you go back to Minnesota?"

"Tonight."

His brows arched. "So soon?"

"I want to get back to Emma." Juliet had deliberately limited her visit to one day. Long enough to accomplish the purpose of her trip. Short enough so that she wouldn't be tempted to do something stupid, like phone Nick from her hotel room.

As if he'd read her mind, he asked, "Weren't you planning to contact me while you were in town?"

"I…didn't even know if you'd be here. Don't you spend most of your time out of the country?"

He nodded. ''I just got back from a mission a couple of days ago.''

''Well. I'm happy to see you made it back in one piece.'' She would never, ever be able to endure the anxiety, the agony and suspense of waiting for Nick to return home from a dangerous, distant assignment. Even picturing something he'd already survived made her stomach churn with terror.

''When does your plane leave?''

''In two hours.''

He seemed disturbed by that, but maybe she was imagining it. *Say something, Nick. Ask me if we can spend those two hours together, ask me to postpone my flight until tomorrow, ask me—*

Juliet slammed a mental door against any further possibilities. Why torture herself, when she would just have to say no?

A chill settled deep in her bones. There was no point in standing out here in the harsh cold any longer, both of them rooted to the ground like a pair of trees, unable or unwilling to bend toward each other.

She took a last look at his face, at those unforgettable eyes that mirrored the steel-gray clouds overhead. And were just as unreachable.

Saying goodbye should be easier the second time.

It wasn't. ''I have to go, Nick.'' Without waiting for his reply, Juliet forced herself to turn, forced her feet to move toward the car.

Then one last question stopped her. She turned around, shoving flyaway hair out of her face. ''Why did you try to call me last night?''

Nick started as if she'd caught him off guard. As if he didn't want to answer. He took his time replying, and when he did, the wind snatched his answer away almost before it reached her.

"I guess I just needed to hear your voice."

She'd half expected an excuse, an evasion, but the simple truth in his confession came through loud and clear. Juliet's breath snagged in her throat. Her heart contracted with a sharp, poignant throb.

Need. Had Nick Ryan ever admitted to needing someone before? She doubted it.

She wasn't sure which one of them moved first. But all at once they were racing toward each other, stumbling over the uneven ground, hands outstretched with eagerness to close the gap between them.

They collided in a violent tangle of arms and legs, of questing hands and seeking mouths. A wave of yearning crashed through Juliet, so intense, it might have knocked her off her feet if Nick hadn't been holding her against him as if he would never let go.

His mouth was hard, urgent, greedy. He plunged his fingers through her hair, tilted back her head to deepen their kiss. Heat ignited in her belly and spread like wildfire, thawing the chill in her bones. From faraway she heard faint, incoherent moans, then realized they were coming from her own throat.

She tightened her arms around his neck with a sudden, overpowering wish that they could strip off their coats and all the clothes beneath them, never mind that they were in a public place with a raw north wind blowing. She ached to be as close to Nick as she could get, as close as a man and a woman could be. For two weeks she'd craved his touch, hungered for the taste and feel and smell of him.

She twined her tongue around his, ran her fingers through his hair, pressed her breasts into the solid wall of his chest. She couldn't believe how good it felt to be back in his arms, to let her passion flow free—the passion she'd tried so hard to dam up ever since he'd left. Kissing him, caressing him, molding her body into his...

It felt so good, so right...only, it *wasn't* right, it was all wrong, and she couldn't let herself fall into the trap of dreaming it could ever be otherwise.

With a strength born of hopelessness and despair, Juliet wrenched herself from their embrace.

Panting, she staggered back a step, swinging up her palm in a warning to Nick. He stayed where he was, but with the watchful, grudging tension of an animal restrained by a leash.

The chill seeped back inside her, even colder and more pervasive than before. "I have to go, Nick."

He clenched his fists. Unclenched them. "Let me drive you to the airport."

"I have a rental car." She pointed vaguely over her shoulder.

"I'll walk you to it, then."

She should have said no, should have run for the refuge of the car as fast as her wobbly legs would carry her. Every additional moment she spent in Nick's presence was a painful reminder of what she'd lost. What they'd both lost.

But wasting energy in argument might drain the last reserves of her dignity. She did not intend to break down and cry in front of Nick.

He walked close beside her, sheltering her from the worst of the wind. Careful not to bump against her.

"You going to be all right?" he asked when her shaky hand finally unlocked and opened the car door.

"Yes." How else could she answer?

"Juliet." She flinched when Nick took her shoulders, rotated her to face him. His stormy, dark expression reflected her own emotional turbulence. "I wish we didn't have to...keep saying goodbye."

She released a sound that veered dangerously close to a sob. "Yes, it's becoming a rather unfortunate habit, isn't it?"

His hold on her tightened. "If only there were some—"

She cut him off by pressing her fingers to his mouth. "If only's don't count for much, do they, Nick?"

Grim acknowledgment flickered in his eyes.

Juliet could hardly doubt Nick had strong feelings for her. Not strong enough, however, to change his life.

Without another word, she slid behind the steering wheel, shut the door, started the car and drove off without looking back. At last the tears flowed, smearing her vision, making the drive on busy, unfamiliar highways even more of a challenge.

The whole way to the airport she felt the hot brand of Nick's mouth on her fingers.

Chapter 14

Nick was hunkered down outside one of the coffee stalls in the marketplace, sipping a demitasse of the local brew that was probably strong enough to etch metal. He didn't care to picture what it might be doing to his insides.

He was dressed to blend in with the crowd, wearing a sand-colored cotton robe that covered him from neck to toe, except his toes were visible through his sandals. His head was protected from the dust and heat by the headdress they called a kaffiyeh.

His disguise probably wouldn't fool any careful observer, but Nick had to admit, it was comfortable. And at least he wouldn't stick out like a sore thumb while waiting for his local contact to show up for their rendezvous.

Normally he would have enjoyed hanging out in the bazaar, a warren of countless stalls offering every item imaginable—colorful rugs, woven blankets, handmade baskets, jewelry, leather and every kind of trashy knickknack you could think of.

The air was saturated with the fragrances of grilled meat and exotic spices, with the loud cries of hawkers, the plaintive wails of beggars, the chatter of customers bickering over prices. Bells jingled as a donkey walked by, laden with goods brought in from the countryside. Live chickens squawked, awaiting their fate in blissful ignorance, while street urchins darted through the crowd like eels.

But all the rich ambience was lost on Nick. His entire life, he'd inhaled foreign atmospheres with the gusto of a swimmer coming up for air. But lately their appeal had dimmed, fading like worn photographs of pleasant memories long in the past.

Instead, he kept thinking about a small town in Minnesota. About Norman Rockwell houses with snow-covered yards and shutters with little hearts cut out of them. About the people who lived in those houses, and how much it had meant to pretend he was one of them for a while.

Seeing Juliet in Washington last week had clinched the fact Nick had suspected. Against all odds, footloose bachelor and confirmed loner Nick Ryan had fallen in love. Hard.

For so long, the concept of settling down had struck him with the same aversion as a life sentence in prison. Now, all he could think about was coming home every night to Juliet and Emma. Sharing meals with them, celebrating holidays together, building a future. A family.

Nick had never been part of a normal family before, never even thought he wanted one. But becoming a temporary part of Juliet's had shown him what he was missing.

And, much to his surprise, the prospect of making love to the same woman for the rest of his life was far more exciting than the lure of far-off horizons or the siren call of adventure. As long as the woman was Juliet.

Maybe creating a family was simply a different kind of adventure. A tougher challenge than Nick had ever faced before.

And at least one thing about him hadn't changed— he still loved a challenge.

He was so absorbed by these speculations, he nearly forgot why he was sitting in the marketplace. He yanked his attention back to his surroundings. He still had a job to do, and no intention of—

He catapulted to his feet. A ragtag bunch of kids, barefoot and noisy, were wrestling over a treasure they'd discovered. Their laughter and the rough way they were handling it proved they didn't have a clue what they were fighting over.

But now they'd gotten close enough for Nick to see its homemade timing device.

He shoved through the mob, seized the object amid indignant yells of protest and took off running, all the while frantically searching for someplace safe to get rid of it. The bazaar was teeming with people.

Then he spotted the well. Instantly he changed course, the crowd of howling kids in hot pursuit.

Nick skidded to a halt, lobbed the object into the opening.

The bomb went off.

"Surprise!"
All five of Carl and Dora Hansen's grandchildren

popped out from behind the sofa in Juliet's living room.

"Happy Birthday, Grampa!"

"We got you presents—"

"And there's cake, too!"

"It's your surprise party!"

Carl goggled at his wife. "Why, Gramma, you told me we were coming over here to take Juliet and Emma to the movies!"

Suzanne grinned at Tim.

Emma tugged on Carl's pant leg. "Were you really s'prised, Grampa?"

He swung her high into the air. "I sure was, sugar-plum."

Juliet motioned her niece Karly. "Want to help me light the candles on the cake?"

"Sure!" Ten-year-old Karly, fellow conspirator, sneaked into the kitchen with her aunt. She frowned at the cake Juliet had baked that morning. "Aren't there s'posed to be sixty-three candles? That's how old Grampa is."

"I know, but the candles would melt before we got them all lit." Juliet finished her task and blew out the match. "Besides, do you know how hard it would be for poor Grampa to blow out sixty-three candles?"

"Oh." Karly nodded wisely. "Then he might not get his wish."

"Instead, I put six candles on this side of the cake, and three on the other."

"Sixty-three!"

"Right!" Juliet gave her niece a one-armed hug. "Want to carry out the cake?"

"Okay!"

As Karly entered the dining room, Tim boomed out the first strains of "Happy Birthday to you…"

They all joined in. "Happy Birthday, dear Grampa…"

While Juliet and Karly had been in the kitchen, someone had passed out the party hats. With exquisite care, Karly set the cake on the table beneath the canopy of blue and yellow crepe paper streamers strung overhead.

"Happy Birthday to you!" Tim pulled the last note up into a screeching falsetto that made the rest of them laugh.

"Blow out the candles, Grampa!"

"Don't forget to make a wish!"

Juliet's father stepped up to the table, rubbed his hands briskly together, pretended to shove up his sleeves and flex his muscles. Dora clicked her tongue and poked him in the ribs. He hauled in an enormous breath…and *blew,* cheeks puffed out like a chipmunk storing up for winter.

The grandkids clapped and cheered and jumped up and down. "You blew them all out, Grampa!"

"What'd you wish for?"

Carl wagged an admonishing finger at Kurt. "Can't tell you that, can I, or I won't get my wish."

"Here, Mommy. Here's your party hat."

"Why, thank you, Tinker Bell." Juliet paused before cutting the cake to adjust the pointy clown hat on her head.

"Want me to get the ice cream?" Suzanne asked on her way to the kitchen.

"Thanks. It's in the freezer." Juliet realized what she'd said and rolled her eyes. "Where else would it be, huh?"

"Well, you could have kept it outside today." Suzanne crossed her arms and shivered. "Brr! I'll sure be glad when spring comes."

"It's only the last day of January. You might have to wait awhile."

"Maybe your brother will give me a nice vacation to Hawaii for Valentine's Day this year," she said, loud enough for Tim to hear.

He blew her a kiss. "I'll keep you warm, my sweet. Not to worry."

Suzanne made a face and disappeared into the kitchen.

Juliet laughed while she cut the first piece of cake. "Whoops, hold on there, Kurt. That one's for Grampa."

Someone knocked on the front door.

Dora was closer. "I'll get it, dear." She motioned Juliet to stay and pass out the rest of the cake while she went to answer it.

"You're s'posed to wait till Grampa starts to eat his," Emma informed Kyle in a loud stage whisper.

Kyle got a guilty look on his face and swallowed.

Juliet licked a dab of chocolate frosting from her thumb. "Okay now, did everyone—"

Her heart leapt to her throat.

Nick was in her living room—and headed straight for her.

The others noticed Juliet's face before they noticed Nick. Heads whirled around to see what on earth could have made her face go white as vanilla ice cream.

Emma let out a squeal of glee. "Uncle Nick! Uncle Nick!" Abandoning her cake, she flew across the dining room.

Juliet's mind reeled with shock, but she knew she would never, ever forget the look on Nick's face when he scooped Emma into his arms. He spun her around, his eyes closed, her arms latched around his neck in a stranglehold.

Finally Emma let go. "You came for Grampa's party," she said happily.

"Couldn't miss that, could I?" Nick cleared his throat and cast a sheepish glance at the rest of the wide-eyed Hansen clan. He tapped Emma's nose. "But I really came 'cause I need to talk to your mommy."

All gazes switched to Juliet. Heat flooded her face. Before she could say anything, Tim stepped forward. "Well, well. This sure is a surprise. How've you been, Ryan? How's the job?" A hint of steel underlay his pleasantries.

Juliet appreciated her big brother's protectiveness, but she needed to handle the situation herself. Now that her initial shock had worn off, she found she could actually move her muscles again. "It's okay, Tim." She curved a hand on his arm.

"Matter of fact, I've got a new job," Nick said casually.

Juliet blinked. "You do?"

"I put in for a transfer to become an instructor of Agency recruits."

"And...what does that mean?" she asked cautiously.

"No more travel, for one thing. Regular hours."

"Sounds less...dangerous."

"Only danger involved will be navigating the D.C. traffic at rush hour."

Juliet was sure there must be a catch. "Won't this new job seem awfully, uh, tame to you?"

"Dazzling a bunch of raw recruits with my vast skill and experience? Training them to make decisions in life-or-death situations? Tame?" He grinned and shook his head. "Heck, no. I can hardly wait."

The strange part was, Juliet believed him. "Maybe...we should talk some more in the kitchen."

"Good idea." He let Emma slide gently to the floor.

"Can I come with you?" she begged, clinging to his leg.

"Not right now, Tinker Bell." Juliet gently detached her daughter. "Uncle Nick and I have to talk by ourselves for a while."

"Better come finish your cake, sweetie pie, before Grampa eats it." Dora gave Juliet an encouraging wink and herded Emma toward the table.

As Juliet passed Suzanne, her sister-in-law whispered, "Your hat."

Quickly Juliet whipped off the silly party hat perched on her head. Nick followed her into the kitchen. Now that she was starting to absorb the amazing fact of his presence, she noticed something that hadn't registered at first.

"Your head!" She touched the white bandage taped just below his hairline. "What happened?"

He hoisted one shoulder. "Just a little bomb, that's all."

"A *bomb?*"

Unfortunately there was no door between the kitchen and dining room. Instead of festive party sounds, dead silence emerged from the other room.

Highly suspicious.

"Come on." Nick captured her wrist.

"Wait! Where are we—"

He grabbed a coat from a hook by the back door. "Juliet, I like your family very much. But I am not going to have this conversation where they can overhear every single word!"

He ushered her into the backyard and shut the door behind them. "Here, put this on."

"Tell me about the bomb." She struggled to shove her arms through the coat sleeves.

"Wasn't much to it. Just some homemade, amateurish device." Nick plowed a trail through the snow until they were well out of eavesdropping range. "I spotted it before it went off and managed to dispose of it before it did any damage."

"Except to you." Juliet uncrossed her arms long enough to point at the bandage.

"I didn't move away quite fast enough. But it was nothing, just a superficial wound."

Juliet's frown conveyed her skepticism. Nick brought his hands to her shoulders. "Okay. Even though it hardly scratched me, when that bomb went off...I'll admit for a split second I thought I was dead. And while I was in the hospital—"

"I thought you said you were barely injured!"

"Nothing that couldn't be patched up by a couple days in the hospital. But it gave me time to think about a lot of things."

"Such as...?"

"My job, for example." Nick's breath steamed out in white puffs. "I started wondering why the hell my job should matter more than anything else. Why did I have to keep putting my career first, just because my parents did?"

Juliet was hardly breathing at all. Everything had gone still inside her.

"A couple months ago, the suggestion that my job shouldn't have top priority would have been unthinkable. But then I met you and Emma, and the rest of your family, and finally I could understand why Brad went to all the trouble of living a double life. Because having a family was worth it to him." Nick gave her shoulders a squeeze. "Because *you* were worth it to him."

"But I wasn't worth giving up his career," Juliet murmured.

Nick rubbed his hands up and down her arms as if to warm her. "Brad wanted it all. And he went to enormous lengths to get it, even lying to the people who meant most to him. But in the end he lost everything." Sorrow darkened Nick's face. "He wound up dead, breaking his wife's heart and leaving behind a child who will never know him."

Juliet felt the pinprick of tears.

Nick coaxed her a little closer. "While I was lying there in that hospital bed, I realized that I don't want to leave the same kind of legacy as my brother." He slid his hands around her waist and pulled her against him. His breath warmed her face while his gaze darted rapidly across hers, as if seeking something. "I love you, Juliet. You and Emma both. I want us to be a real family."

A flame leapt to life inside her, spreading flickering tendrils of heat.

"Marry me, Juliet. Please be my wife."

The heat rose higher inside her, but it carried doubt along with it. Hadn't it been just weeks ago that she'd sworn she could never trust a man again, not after discovering how Brad had betrayed her?

Yet she'd also been convinced she would never love another man again, either. And boy, oh, boy, she'd certainly been wrong about that.

She'd believed Nick was just like his brother. But hadn't he just proved he wasn't, by giving up his dangerous job, by making the sacrifice for her that Brad wouldn't?

Maybe trusting someone always involved risk. But now Juliet realized how much there was to lose by refusing to take that risk, by refusing to listen to your heart.

Juliet listened to her heart. And heard the answer.

"Sweetheart," Nick urged through teeth clamped together to keep from chattering, "please. Hurry up and answer, before we both freeze out here."

Juliet laughed and threw her arms around his neck. "That's one of the things I love about you, Nick Ryan. You're so practical."

"Then...you do love me, right?" For once in his life he sounded unsure of himself.

Juliet brought her smile an inch from his mouth. "Nick Ryan, I am completely, thoroughly, one-hundred-percent, head over heels in love with—"

She didn't quite get to finish her sentence.

Their kiss could have melted the icicles off the eaves. A blizzard of joy and desire swirled through Juliet as Nick hugged her hard enough to lift her off her toes.

Finally they had to break apart so they could breathe. "My goodness," she gasped.

Nick kept his arms wrapped securely, possessively around her. "So, does this mean you'll marry me?"

He sounded pretty confident, but Juliet could tell he wasn't going to be completely sure of himself until she made it official.

She nuzzled her nose against his. Both were cold as ice. "Yes," she said softly, looking deep into his eyes. "That's what it means."

After a dazed heartbeat or two, Nick threw back his head and let out a whoop of triumph. Then he swept up Juliet and whirled her around and around till they both nearly toppled into the snow.

Laughing, she staggered upright and linked her arm through his. "Come on. We'd better go back inside."

"Your lips are blue," he told her. "Want me to warm them up?"

"Later." She tugged him toward the house. "First my teeth have to stop chattering, or we might have an unfortunate accident."

"I love you," he said.

"I love you, too." Happiness spiraled through her, strong and pure and radiant. She couldn't seem to stop smiling, and not because her face was frozen.

Then the first pang of separation hit her. Marrying Nick meant moving to Washington. He'd made an enormous change in his life for her, and it was only fair that Juliet do the same for him. Which meant leaving behind the family she'd lived so close to all her life. The family she'd loved and depended on, whose daily presence she knew she would sorely miss.

The family who, at this exact moment, was spying on her and Nick through Emma's bedroom window.

"Uh-oh." Nick nudged her ribs when he spotted them, too. "Think they saw everything?"

Juliet groaned. Judging by the crowd of smug, excited faces beaming from the window, they certainly had. She gave them a sassy wave.

Her darling Emma, she was delighted to note, wore the biggest smile of all.

Epilogue

The following Christmas Eve

Nick grumbled behind his curly white beard. "I can't believe I let your brother trick me into playing Santa Claus again this year."

Juliet adjusted the red cap on top of his head and stepped back to check the results. "Looks like it's becoming a tradition." She gave Nick one of those knockout smiles that still made him marvel over how incredibly lucky he was to have her for his wife. "Hmm." A frown marred her beautiful brow. "That hat looks a little crooked...."

When she stepped close to straighten it, Nick took the opportunity to grab her and whisk her onto his lap, plunking them both down on the edge of the bed.

They were upstairs in her parents' room just like last year, having flown in from Washington three days ago. Juliet laughed and pretended to push Nick away, but nevertheless wound up cuddled against him, arms draped around his neck.

"And what would you like for Christmas this year, young lady?" he boomed in a gruff Santa voice, bouncing her on his knee.

"Shh!" Juliet clapped a hand over his mouth, but she was laughing. "The kids will hear you downstairs!"

"Oops!" Nick lowered his voice. "What would Emma say if she came up here and found Mommy kissing Santa Claus, huh?" He settled his arms around Juliet. "Well, if you won't tell me what presents you'd like, then Santa will break tradition and tell you the present *he* wants. Maybe for next Christmas."

A secret smile played around her lips. "Okay, Santa. What's your wish?"

This red suit was getting hot. Nick ran a finger beneath his collar. "Now, I don't want you getting the wrong idea. I mean, you know I love Emma like she was my own, even before I adopted her this summer."

"I know." Juliet's eyes softened.

"But I was thinking, wouldn't it be nice, maybe, if pretty soon we...added on to our family?"

Juliet pressed a pensive finger to her chin and looked puzzled. "You mean get a puppy, the way Emma's always begging to?"

Nick gritted his teeth. "No, I am not talking about a dog!" Now he was really starting to sweat. "I'm talking about a baby! *Our* baby, yours and mine! A little brother or sister for Emma. Is that such a crazy—"

Juliet leaned over and whispered in his ear.

Nick's white eyebrows jumped toward the ceiling. "You're *what?*" He seized her arms and pushed her back to see her face.

It was luminous. She said, almost shyly, "I was going to save the news—"

"When?" Nick's grip tightened.

"Well, for New Year's Eve, when the two of us would be alone so we could—"

He interrupted with a hysterical chuckle. "No, no, I mean, when is the baby coming?"

"Oh." Her mouth curved happily. "Late July."

Nick stared at her. A strange, overwhelming feeling started deep inside him, collected strength and quickly filled his entire being until he could barely contain it. He wanted to holler from the rooftops, run laps around the lake, dance an Irish jig until dawn.

Instead, he slid his arms around his wife and kissed her as tenderly as he could with that roller-coaster rush zooming around inside him.

She was so sweet…so exciting…the love of his life.

After a while, Juliet broke off their kiss with a giggle. "Santa," she murmured, "your beard tickles."

"Ho, ho, ho," Nick said. Then he kissed her again anyway.

* * * * *

If you enjoyed what you just read,
then we've got an offer you can't resist!

Take 2 bestselling love stories FREE!

Plus get a FREE surprise gift!

Clip this page and mail it to Silhouette Reader Service™

IN U.S.A.	IN CANADA
3010 Walden Ave.	P.O. Box 609
P.O. Box 1867	Fort Erie, Ontario
Buffalo, N.Y. 14240-1867	L2A 5X3

YES! Please send me 2 free Silhouette Intimate Moments® novels and my free surprise gift. Then send me 6 brand-new novels every month, which I will receive months before they're available in stores. In the U.S.A., bill me at the bargain price of $3.57 plus 25¢ delivery per book and applicable sales tax, if any*. In Canada, bill me at the bargain price of $3.96 plus 25¢ delivery per book and applicable taxes**. That's the complete price and a savings of over 10% off the cover prices—what a great deal! I understand that accepting the 2 free books and gift places me under no obligation ever to buy any books. I can always return a shipment and cancel at any time. Even if I never buy another book from Silhouette, the 2 free books and gift are mine to keep forever. So why not take us up on our invitation. You'll be glad you did!

245 SEN CNFF
345 SEN CNFG

Name		(PLEASE PRINT)	
Address		Apt.#	
City		State/Prov.	Zip/Postal Code

* Terms and prices subject to change without notice. Sales tax applicable in N.Y.
** Canadian residents will be charged applicable provincial taxes and GST.
   All orders subject to approval. Offer limited to one per household.
   ® are registered trademarks of Harlequin Enterprises Limited.

INMOM99   ©1998 Harlequin Enterprises Limited

Don't miss Silhouette's newest cross-line promotion,

Four royal sisters find their own Prince Charmings as they embark on separate journeys to find their missing brother, the Crown Prince!

Royally Wed

The search begins in October 1999 and continues through February 2000:

On sale October 1999: **A ROYAL BABY ON THE WAY**
by award-winning author **Susan Mallery** (Special Edition)

On sale November 1999: **UNDERCOVER PRINCESS**
by bestselling author **Suzanne Brockmann** (Intimate Moments)

On sale December 1999: **THE PRINCESS'S WHITE KNIGHT**
by popular author **Carla Cassidy** (Romance)

On sale January 2000: **THE PREGNANT PRINCESS**
by rising star **Anne Marie Winston** (Desire)

On sale February 2000: **MAN...MERCENARY...MONARCH**
by top-notch talent **Joan Elliott Pickart** (Special Edition)

ROYALLY WED
Only in—
SILHOUETTE BOOKS

Available at your favorite retail outlet.

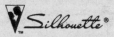

Visit us at www.romance.net

SSERW

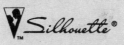

Start celebrating Silhouette's 20th anniversary
with these 4 special titles by
New York Times bestselling authors

Fire and Rain
by Elizabeth Lowell

King of the Castle
by Heather Graham Pozzessere

State Secrets
by Linda Lael Miller

Paint Me Rainbows
by Fern Michaels

On sale in December 1999

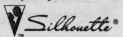

Celebrate Silhouette's 20th Anniversary

With beloved authors, exciting new miniseries and special keepsake collections, **plus** the chance to enter our 20th anniversary contest, in which one lucky reader wins the trip of a lifetime!

Take a look at who's celebrating with us:

DIANA PALMER

April 2000: SOLDIERS OF FORTUNE
May 2000 in Silhouette Romance: *Mercenary's Woman*

NORA ROBERTS

May 2000: IRISH HEARTS, the 2-in-1 keepsake collection
June 2000 in Special Edition: *Irish Rebel*

LINDA HOWARD

July 2000: MacKENZIE'S MISSION
August 2000 in Intimate Moments: *A Game of Chance*

ANNETTE BROADRICK

October 2000: a special keepsake collection, plus a brand-new title in
November 2000 in Desire

Available at your favorite retail outlet.

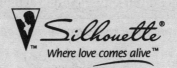

EXTRA! EXTRA!

The book all your favorite authors are raving about is finally here!

The 1999 Harlequin and Silhouette coupon book.

Each page is alive with savings that can't be beat!

Getting this incredible coupon book is as easy as 1, 2, 3.

1. During the months of November and December 1999 buy any 2 Harlequin or Silhouette books.

2. Send us your name, address and 2 proofs of purchase (cash receipt) to the address below.

3. Harlequin will send you a coupon book worth $10.00 off future purchases of Harlequin or Silhouette books in 2000.

Send us 3 cash register receipts as proofs of purchase and we will send you 2 coupon books worth a total saving of $20.00 (limit of 2 coupon books per customer).

Saving money has never been this easy.

Please allow 4-6 weeks for delivery. Offer expires December 31, 1999.

I accept your offer! Please send me (a) coupon booklet(s):

Name: _____

Address: _____ City: _____

State/Prov.: _____ Zip/Postal Code: _____

Send your name and address, along with your cash register receipts as proofs of purchase, to:

In the U.S.: Harlequin Books, P.O. Box 9057, Buffalo, N.Y. 14269

In Canada: Harlequin Books, P.O. Box 622, Fort Erie, Ontario L2A 5X3

Order your books and accept this coupon offer through our web site
http://www.romance.net
Valid in U.S. and Canada only.   PHQ4994R